Maggie's Secrets

Nancy Evelyn Allen

MACE Publishing—Nolensville, TN
ISBN: 979-8-9857788-0-9
Library of Congress Control Number: 2022903559
Title: Maggie's Secrets
Author: Nancy Evelyn Allen
Digital distribution | 2022
Paperback | 2022

Acknowledgments

My humble appreciation and thanks go out to so many people who encouraged and helped me with this book: First to my husband who suffered through every version and rewrite, and to all the people who read and offered their advice and comments, especially Chris Allen and Judy Hagar.

Chapter 1

Maggie awoke to the phone ringing. She looked at the clock and jumped out of bed. It was 8:00 a.m. She usually got up at seven. She must have really been tired.

"Hello, oh hello Daddy. I wasn't even up yet. How're you this morning?"

"I'm doing alright. Just checking on you to see if you got your meat in the freezer and if you got home alright? Did you hear from Tom?"

"Yep, meat is all packed away and no, I didn't get a letter. I know he's busy. I just need to be patient."

"I allow maybe he's alright. Don't worry. If you need to talk . . .

Maggie cut in, "Daddy, I know you love me. Tom will write when he's ready. It's hard to talk about."

"You're strong. You'll be fine. I'll call tomorrow," said Avery.

"Bye, Daddy. I love you," said Maggie, hanging up the phone and sinking to the floor. *I just feel something is wrong, but what? I'm just being selfish. Just get up and make yourself some breakfast. You'll feel better after you get something in your stomach.* The cereal box shook as she poured Cornflakes into her bowl. She spilled the milk on the table and a few drops on the floor. She took her cereal over to the television and turned it on. The news blared loud. Her first impulse was to turn it off, but "there have been casualties in Vietnam. Three American soldiers have been killed," said the news reporter. "Their names have not been released pending notification of their next of kin." Maggie sat dumbfounded. *Could one of them be Tom?* She prayed "no, Lord don't let it be Tom." *It's not him*, she told herself. *I would have been notified by now.* She picked up her bowl and headed to the kitchen. *Not much dishes to wash when you cook for one*, she thought, as she rinsed the bowl and left it in the drainer.

Maggie headed up the stairs to dress. She would go for a run and shower when she returned, but as she reached to open the front door the doorbell rang.

"Good morning, officers?" said Maggie.

"Good morning," said Captain Murphy. "Are you Mrs. Tom Adams?"

"Yes, that's right. Is Tom alright?" asked Maggie.

"Well, ma'am, that's what we're here about."

"Come in," she said, as they walked into the living room and sat down on the sofa.

"Your husband died two days ago when the North Vietnamese guerrillas raided his living quarters in Saigon. He and two other United States officers were completely surprised by their attack," said Captain Murphy.

"Wait. Are you telling me Tom is dead?" asked Maggie.

"Lieutenant Adams made the ultimate sacrifice for his country," said Sergeant Henry. "We offer our most sincere condolences."

Maggie sat staring at the floor. "Condolences? What good are condolences? Condolences won't bring my husband back to me," she screamed.

"No ma'am, we understand. We're sorry. I wish I could bring him back to you," said Captain Murphy.

Maggie sat silent for over a minute before Captain Murphy spoke again. "To which funeral home would you want us to tell the Army to send your husband's body?"

"Smith/Johnson, I guess. Tom's parents live here and they have a burial plot."

Maggie was silent, thoughts racing through her head. *I'll need to notify Tom's parents and my parents and my school. I'll take a few days off from school to get things together.* She sat with her hands folded and her head down.

"Again, we're sorry for your loss," said Captain Murphy, as he stood to leave. "The funeral home will call you when the body arrives so you can make arrangements. Lieutenant Adams will be eligible for a military funeral if you want one. The funeral home will know how to get that done."

"Right now, I don't know what I want," said Maggie.

"I understand," said Captain Murphy, as he opened the front door to leave.

Maggie's eyes were a blur. Her thoughts mangled; her hands numb. *How could Tom die?* She channeled her thoughts toward the children--her first-grade class. *Who would replace the child that moved? How can I manage the little boys who are so hyperactive? And the little girl who cries and seems to never speak? How can I build trust in my students?* When she looked up it was three in the afternoon. "I must call Tom's parents," she said aloud as she came back to reality and reached for the phone.

"Mrs. Adams," said Maggie.

"Oh, hi Maggie, I've been meaning to call you. How are you?"

"I have bad news," said Maggie. "A couple of officers from the Army came by a little while ago and told me. Tom is dead. He and two of his fellow officers were taken by surprise and killed by North Vietnamese guerrillas."

There was silence on the other end of the phone.

"Mrs. Adams?" said Maggie.

"I'm here, I just don't know what to say," said Mrs. Adams.

"His body will be sent to Smith/Johnson Funeral Home and they'll let us know when we can make the arrangements," said Maggie. "I have to make some more calls. I love you. I'll call you as soon as I learn anything."

"Ok, do you want us to come to your house tonight?"

"No, we can get together tomorrow," said Maggie. "I'll call."

"You take care of yourself," said Mrs. Adams.

"You, too," said Maggie."

Maggie didn't want to call her daddy. She wanted him to hold her and make it better. The telephone seemed so cold. But it was already 4:30 in the afternoon. It was too late to ask him to come to Durant. He had milking to do and the animals to care for. He might even already be at the barn. Maggie sat remembering how her daddy had always kept her safe, even putting her down in the bib of his overalls, where she stood on his legs when they rode the horse to bring the cows in from the back pasture. She felt his love as she picked up the phone to call her parents' number in Boonetown. The phone range five times before her mother answered.

"Hello," said Lucy.

"Hi, Mother. Is Daddy there?"

"He's at the barn. He's trying to get through early. We're going out to eat with our friends. Do you want something? I need to get dressed."

"Yes, Mother, I need to tell you something. Tom is dead. He was killed by the North Vietnamese."

"I knew you shouldn't have married that man. He's never been right for you. I just can't stand it when these kinds of things happen. It makes me jittery," said Lucy.

"You're right. I shouldn't have married Tom, but I was 23 years old and all I could hear was I was going to be an old maid," said Maggie.

"You could have married that nice boy, Jim. He wanted to date you, but you wouldn't go out with him," said Lucy. "I guess you'll want us to come to Durant. I never plan anything that I don't have to give it up," said Lucy.

"Mother, it's alright. Don't worry. I'll be fine. I don't need you to come. Just tell Daddy I'll call him tomorrow."

"I'm so tore up now, I probably won't be able to enjoy my dinner," said Lucy.

"Mother, calm down. I'll talk to you tomorrow."

Maggie phoned her principal and told him she would have to take the next week off.

Exhausted and alone, Maggie decided to check the mailbox. There was a letter from Tom. *How could this happen? Why would I get a letter from Tom just after I've been told he's dead? This is all a cruel dream. I'll wake up and it'll be over. I can't do this.* Maggie laid the letter on the coffee table, turned the TV on and sat down on the couch. The news reporter was talking about the drug problem in Durant. *That doesn't have anything to do with me.* she thought, as she turned the TV off and picked up Tom's letter. She sat with the letter in her hand for several minutes before she opened it. *This man whom I barely know has written me his final letter. What do I know about him? He' dead. We married on the run. I had known him for three months when we married and two months later, he was shipped out. There was not enough time. Why did this happen?* Maggie unfolded the paper. The letter was printed in Tom's neatest handwriting:

Dear Maggie,

It's cold here and raining. Infantrymen are always cold, but the guys are great. There's not much happening. I can't say much. I just want you to know I miss you. When I'm home, we'll make up for lost time. Tell your daddy and my parents hello for me. I don't have time to write letters.
Love,
Tom

Maggie read the letter three times before she laid it back on the coffee table where it remained for the next two weeks.

Chapter 2

After the funeral Maggie spent a day and a half with her parents. At the funeral Avery had invited her to move back home. It was comforting, but she knew it was not the right thing. She would never be able to go back and live with her parents. She had to make a life for herself and her life was in Durant.

"Tom was a good man. I'm sorry he's gone," said Avery.

"It's not like we were together for a long time. He was shipped out right after we married. If I had known he would be deployed to Vietnam and I couldn't go with him I would have waited to marry. I can't imagine what it would be like for you or mother if one of you passed away.

"Yep, twenty-nine years is a long time. I reckon you get mighty used to someone if you've been with them that long," said Avery. "Your mother was only sixteen when we married and I wasn't very grown-up either. We've grown-up together."

"Tom and I didn't even have the privilege of getting to know each other before he left. I received his last letter the day I was informed of his death."

"Did he say anything significant?" asked Avery.

"Just that things were boring and when they fixed the mess over there we would make up for lost time. I don't really understand why he had to go over there in the first place. You know he wouldn't be allowed to write about what was really happening," said Maggie.

"One of my friends from World War II said one time he wrote a letter to his family telling them all about his location and how the fighting was going. He found himself dressed down by the 'brass'. They said he was endangering the troops," said Avery.

"Yeah, I always kept that in mind. I never expected Tom to tell me much." said Maggie.

"Did you hear about the man from Durant who gave George Anderson a new redbone coon dog?" asked Avery. "George brought him over the other night and we took him hunting with Banjo. They ran good together. We're taking them to the time-trials the end of May. John Butcher told us Banjo has a chance to win. Can you imagine that? I might have a state champion coon hound!"

"What makes you think John Butcher knows? You've always known how to train a dog. Remember Rowdy? I heard you tell that during the Depression the hides you sold from hunting kept food on your table.

"Yeah, Rowdy was a mighty good dog. When that fellow from Alabama offered me three-hundred-dollars for her, I had to take it. Three-hundred-dollars was like a gold mine during the Depression," said Avery.

"Who is this John Butcher fellow, anyway?" asked Maggie.

"Oh, John Butcher is a 'big shot' from Durant. He's some kind of state congressman. I thought you might have heard of him," said Avery. "He and some other fellows have been coming out here going hunting and for some reason they want me to go with them. I guess they've heard about the dogs I've trained. Their dogs are just average, but when they're put with Banjo, they come alive."

Don't guess I pay much attention to politics," said Maggie. "Don't have much dealings anymore with coon dogs either."

"I guess I've trained more dogs and more young hunters than anybody around here. It just hurts to see them go. I even took Nigger Joe's boy, Junior, hunting with me several times. He seemed like a fine young man, but I hear he's into drugs. He got arrested. He's in some place they call The Farm," said Avery. "With all Joe and I shared growing up I feel obligated to try and find out what's happening to Junior."

"I've actually heard of The Farm. If I hear anything about Junior, I'll let you know. I wonder where he got drugs. You wouldn't think a little place like Boonetown would have drugs," said Maggie.

"Young people get around now days. No telling where he got the drugs. It just seems like he's been at The Farm a long time. I've heard it takes about three months to get shed of the habit. He's been there, I guess, about a year now," said Avery.

"You know, The Farm is not just a drug rehab place. It's also a prison. It depends on what he was sent up for. If he was just taking drugs his sentence would be less, but if he was peddling drugs that's a different story," said Maggie.

"I just hope he's alright. One of these days when we have time, I'll tell you a secret Joe and I share. Well, there's more than one, but this one involves you and Junior," said Avery.

"I really do need to get back to Durant, but I'll look forward to hearing about one of your and Joe's secrets from your childhood. That sounds like fun. I have to go back to school tomorrow. I think I may have a new student to replace the one that moved. I need to get a good night's sleep so I'll be on top of things," said Maggie.

"I don't want to hold you up. You should get home before night. I don't like the idea of you being out by herself after dark," said Avery. "There's too much meanness going on."

"I'll be careful. When Mother gets back tell her bye for me," said Maggie as she drove off toward Durant determined to face her new life without Tom.

Maggie found it hard to focus. Her head hurt. She took an aspirin and went to bed early, but crazy dreams plagued her night. She opened her eyes and yawned. It was time to get up. The visit from the Army officers, the funeral and the people who came to pay their respects all seemed like a dream. *But it's not a dream. It's real. Tom is dead. I can't think about him now. I will concentrate on my class. They're my kids and every one of them is special.* She wondered who the new child would be and she was already making plans for him or her. She secretly hoped it would be a girl. She already had eleven boys.

Maggie dressed in a hurry and sped off to school. She wanted to be there early to straighten up her room and prepare for the day. When she arrived only the janitor greeted her. He was a pleasant young black man about her age.

"I'm sorry about your husband," the janitor said.

"Thank you. Does everyone here know what happened?" asked Maggie.

"Well, yes ma'am. Word gets around," he said.

"How did my kids fair with the substitute last week?" Maggie asked.

"They was pretty noisy, but I reckon they survived," he said. "I sorta straightened up your room, but I knew you'd want to put everything back yourself, so I didn't presume to know where things went."

"That's good. I won't have to spend all day looking for stuff." They both laughed.

Maggie went to Room 6 and began collecting materials for her first reading class. The children's nametags were on the wrong desk. She had just finished organizing her room when she noticed a man and a little girl walking down the hall. She stepped outside her door.

"May I help you find something?" Maggie asked.

"Yes, we're looking for Room 6," as he looked up to see the number on the door. "I believe the teacher's name is Mrs. Maggie Adams," said the man.

"You've come to the right place," said. Maggie, extending her hand, "I'm Maggie Adams."

"I'm Brian Scott and this is Mary Alice Scott."

"I'm glad to meet you both," said Maggie, smiling at Mary Alice, as Mary Alice ducked behind her daddy's leg.

"I came in last week and filled out papers," said Brian Scott.

"I'm so sorry. I've been out on personal leave. When I came in this morning I didn't even check with my principal. I was anxious to get to my room and get it organized for the day," said Maggie.

The principal stuck his head in the door. "I see you've met," he said. "Here are Mary Alice's records," handing Maggie a folder.

"I'll make sure I read every word just as soon as I get a break," said Maggie. The children were beginning to file in. "Good Morning, Mrs. Maggie, Good Morning, Good Morning. The children were laughing and greeting each other.

"We have a complicated situation. It's not thoroughly explained in the folder, but perhaps you'll understand and we can talk later," said Mr. Scott.

"Daddy, don't leave me," cried Mary Alice, hanging on to her daddy's hand.

"Mary Alice, you know Daddy has to go to work. Mrs. Adams will take good care of you and you'll be fine. When school is over, I'll be back."

"You promise? I miss Mommy. I'm afraid you won't come back," said Mary Alice.

"I know, sweetheart. I miss Mommy, too. I promise, cross my heart, I'll pick you up when school is over. I love you," said Mr. Scott.

"I love you, too," said Mary Alice, still crying. Brian Scott turned and left the room with the principal.

Maggie took Mary Alice by the hand and led her to the empty desk where she sat with her head down. Maggie wanted to spend more time with Mary Alice, but it was time to begin the day.

The room was full, all the children present. Maggie started by introducing Mary Alice as the new student and all the children greeted her with a loud 'welcome'. Mary Alice didn't respond. Maggie went over and took Mary Alice by the hand. "Come with me, you can help me turn the pages," but Maggie read the story and turned the pages without her help. She appeared to be a very sad little girl.

Mary Alice never smiled, not even when two of the children tried to get her to join them in play. She ate only a few bites of her sandwich at lunch. Maggie asked her about her family, but Mary Alice put her head on the desk and began to cry again. When the day was finally finished, Mr. Scott was at the door. Mary Alice ran to him. "Daddy, you did come back," she said.

"I told you I would be here. You are my sweetheart. I love you and I will never leave you," said Mr. Scott, turning toward Maggie. "How did she do?"

"She's been quiet, but cooperative. I didn't have a chance to study her file, but I'll take it home with me," said Maggie.

"Tell Mrs. Maggie good-bye," said Mr. Scott. Mary Alice turned toward Maggie with her head down and whispered, "bye."

Chapter 3

Maggie laid the folder on the kitchen counter. She was too tired to cook anything. She had ice cream in the freezer. *Yes, ice cream would be just what I need, comfort.* As she began eating, she reached for the folder. *What? What is going on? The words are almost all inked out. Name?* she thought, as she stared at the black ink. *Parent's names? Black ink.* The only information available was Mary Alice's test scores. Maggie was speaking aloud. She reads at the third-grade level. Her math skills are second term first-grade. I'll put her in the accelerated reading group. *But what is going on with this child?* Maggie heard her say, "I miss mommy." *Where is her mother? Why did Mary Alice or whatever her name is transfer schools just before Christmas?* Maggie wondered about Mr. Scott. *Was that his real name? Would he be forthcoming with information?* Maggie would try to make an appointment to talk to him personally before school began. He appeared to not want to talk in front of Mary Alice. Perhaps Maggie should talk to her principal and arrange for an aide to help with the children while she and Mr. Scott talked. Whatever the situation, Maggie knew she needed to be careful not to hurt this precious little girl any more than she had been hurt already. Maggie had no way to contact Mr. Scott. She would have to wait until he arrived with Mary Alice the next day. Maggie scooped up another generous helping of ice cream and curled up on the couch to watch 'I Love Lucy'.

Morning came in with thunder and lightning. It would have been wonderful just to turn over and go back to sleep, but Maggie wanted to meet with Mr. Scott as soon as possible. Cereal was quick and becoming a habit. She promised herself to make a real breakfast, as her daddy would say, on the weekend. Or maybe she would spend the weekend with her parents and let her mother make the breakfast. She made the best biscuits.

Maggie rushed into the school building just as the principal arrived. "Do you have a minute to talk?" asked Maggie.

"Sure, come on in," said the principal, pointing to a chair in front of his desk. "Have a seat. What can I do for you?"

"I guess you know almost all of my new student's record is inked out. Do you know why?"

"I don't know much. I think it has something to do with Mr. Scott's job," said the principal.

"Do you know what his job is?"

"Not exactly, just that he works for the government," said the principal. "I really don't know much else. The school board called and said Mary Alice would be transferring here and it's a special case and we are not to ask too many questions," said the principal.

"Do you think it will be alright if I have a talk with Mr. Scott? Can you provide an aide to sit in with my class if he has time this morning?" asked Maggie.

"Yeah, I'll send one of the girls your way as soon as I see him come in with Mary Alice.

"What do you think is going on?" she asked.

"I honestly don't know, but I think it's serious and we need to abide by Mr. Scott's request," said the principal.

"Thank you for your time," said Maggie, as she turned to go to her room.

Maggie eyed the clock. Mr. Scott and Mary Alice were late, but just as she started the morning calendar they came in, Mary Alice clinging to her daddy's hand.

"Go sit on the carpet with the other children," said Mr. Scott.

"Can you stay with me?" asked Mary Alice.

"No Daddy has to go to work," said Mr. Scott.

An aide stuck her head in the door. "Did you want me to fill in for a while?" she asked.

"Yes, we just started the calendar," said Maggie, as she rose to greet Mr. Scott.

"Do you have a few minutes to talk?" Maggie asked.

"Sure, can we talk somewhere outside?"

"I have arranged for the conference room. It's three doors down on the right. I'll be right there," said Maggie.

Maggie went over and led Mary Alice to the carpet. "I'm going to talk to your daddy for a few minutes. I won't be long."

Mary Alice nodded, as Maggie hurried out the door.

Mr. Scott was waiting in the conference room. Maggie took the seat opposite him. "Mr. Scott, I suppose you know, Mary Alice's records didn't tell me much. I don't even have an address or a contact phone number," began Maggie.

"I'll give you a phone number, taking out a small piece of paper, scribbling a number and handing it to Maggie. It's on a secure line, so it will be alright to call me.

"Thank you. That's something at least," said Maggie. "Can you tell me about her mother?"

"She's missing and that's all I can tell you," said Mr. Scott.

"The principal said you work for the government?"

"Yes, that's right, I work at The Farm."

"The Farm. . . My daddy asked me if I knew anything about The Farm. His friend's son has been there for almost a year. He's a young black man. His name is Junior Joseph. Do you know him?"

"I've seen him and I've talked to him once. I think they call him J.J. I'll check in on him and let you know how he's doing."

"Thank you," said Maggie. "Can you tell me anything else about Mary Alice?"

"She's smart and very emotional since her mother left. It's hard being daddy and mother. She seems to like you," said Mr. Scott.

"She's a beautiful child. I don't have any children and I claim all my students as my own. I'll trust you to tell me what you can. The more I understand, the more I'll be able to help," said Maggie.

"Thank you," said Mr. Scott, as he and Maggie shook hands and left the conference room.

When Maggie entered the classroom, Mary Alice smiled. The day went well. As a matter of fact, the remainder of the week went well. Mary Alice stayed close to Maggie, but she participated in her reading group and even played with a couple of the children at recess. Maggie felt good about their progress.

The Farm

Stan Turner, also known as, Brian Scott, Chester Moore, Bill Tweed, James Therman, Max Tanner and other aliases was assigned a desk at The Farm to provide him a cover while he investigated drug activity in Kentucky. The Farm had been created by the government in order to treat drug addicts. It was not only a prison, but a rehabilitation and research center. When an addict was arrested, he or she was sent to The Farm, but addicts could also admit themselves. The Farm served over eight-hundred inmates who literally farmed over a thousand acres. The male inmates did the farm labor while the female inmates took care of the laundry, cleaning and cooking. The operation was self-sufficient, complete with sports teams, bowling alley, art therapy and music. The idea was if a person got enough fresh air and worked hard, was treated well and given therapy, they would recover from drug addiction.

The CIA was in charge of The Farm and Stan was familiar with most of the employees and most of the activities happening at The Farm. His old friend and mentor, Jeff Newman, was his undercover boss and CEO of The Farm. Stan had worked himself up and was an officer in the CIA, third from the top, with many operatives working under him. He was often sent out of the country. Not even his wife or daughter knew what his work entailed. The only people who knew he was in the CIA was Jeff Newman and other CIA operatives, his friend and lawyer, J. Morris Higgins and the county sheriff. Stan trusted them completely.

Stan had contacted Junior Joseph after Maggie told him he was the son of her daddy's friend. Junior seemed standoffish and leery of Stan. It appeared Junior might have information, so Stan made an appointment to see him again. Junior would be beneficial to his investigation into drug trafficking in Durant, and now Boonetown. Why would Boonetown be involved? If he could get Junior to trust him, maybe he would tell him where he got his drugs. It must be from someone in Boonetown, but who? Everyone seemed so innocent. He could almost count the number of people in Boonetown on his fingers and toes. He had all their names and addresses on a board in his office. Who was it that tied them together? How were they tied to Durant where the drug problem was rampant? Heroin was the drug of choice, but LSD was beginning to edge its way in. Most of the boys at The Farm were on heroin. Brian had questioned many of them from Durant but had never spoken to Junior about his addiction until today.

"Good Morning, Mr. Joseph," said Stan. "How's life treating you?"

"Not bad. My head's clear today," said Junior.

"When I mentioned I was working at The Farm my daughter's teacher said her daddy knew somebody here. She made me promise to watch out for you," said Stan. "So, how're they treating you, really?"

"Well, I don't know. I reckon they're treating me alright. I don't know exactly how I'm supposed to be treated. One day I'm up and the next day I'm down. Don't seem like the medication they're giving me is working very well, but I did volunteer for them to try different things. I really do want to get clean," said Junior.

"If you'll trust me, I'll try and help you," said Stan. "I don't know what your method of treatment has been, but I'll find out. Mrs. Adams has been a good friend to my little girl, so a friend of hers is a friend of mine."

"Me and Mrs. Adams ain't exactly friends," said Junior. It's our daddies that know each other."

"Mrs. Adams wants the best for you," said Stan. "I'm here to help you."

"I don't want to cause any trouble or get anybody else in trouble," said Junior.

"Don't worry about that. What's said between you and me will stay between you and me," said Stan.

"I don't have anything to tell you," said Junior.

"I understand. I'm not pressuring you, but if you ever want to talk, you know I'm here," said Stan.

"I hear you, but I don't need to talk," said Junior.

"I understand. You have a good rest of the day and I'll check in on you right after Christmas. I hear they're having a big Christmas music festival on Saturday. Do you like music?" asked Stan.

"Yeah, my daddy leads music at church and he taught me how to play the banjo. He never had lessons. He just picked it up naturally.

They have a banjo here in the music room. I play every now and again. I'll probably go if I'm feeling up to it," said Junior.

"Well, ok than. I'll see you the week after Christmas. Take care of yourself," shaking hands with Junior.

Chapter 4

"Hey Daddy, do you and Mother have anything planned for tomorrow night?" asked Maggie.

"Nothing that I know of," said Avery.

"Then I think I'll come up there and spend the night. I've been craving Mother's ham and biscuit breakfast," said Maggie.

"Come right ahead. We'll love to have you," said Avery.

Maggie slept until eight o'clock. It was her best night's sleep since Tom died. She couldn't help but lie in bed and wonder what their life together would have been like. *Would they have had children? He was handsome and resourceful. If he had stayed in the military, they would have traveled.* Maggie had not even been out of the state. She had never been on an airplane or a train for that matter. She had never seen the ocean.

Cornflakes was an alright breakfast, but tomorrow ham and biscuits would be better. She sat down on the couch to eat. Eating at the table made her feel alone. Just as she took the first bite the phone rang.

"Hello," said Maggie.

"Hello, this is Brian Scott. I hope I'm not calling too early.

"No, it's not too early. I've been up for a while," said Maggie.

"Mary Alice and I are going to the park today for a picnic. I told her we would have to wear our snowsuits and take hot soup because it's cold out there."

"How cold is it? I haven't been out," said Maggie.

"It's in the forties," said Brian. "We won't stay long. It's the only thing Mary Alice has asked to do in a while. She asked if you could come with us?"

"I wish I could. I'm so sorry. I promised my daddy I would spend the afternoon and night with him. I would love to go. Please tell Mary Alice I promise I'll go next time," said Maggie.

"I hope I'm not out of line asking. It's just you're the first woman Mary Alice has taken to since her mother left. She brightens up when she's with you."

"No, you're not out of line. I'll do anything to help make Mary Alice feel more secure.

"Have fun with your dad, looks like it's going to snow. Be careful out there," said Brian Scott.

"Oh, I'm used to driving in the snow. I'll be careful," said Maggie, as they hung up the phone.

The misty rain was beginning to change into snow. Maggie stared out the window; yes, small flecks of occasional snow were beginning to fall. She grabbed her warm sweats and her big coat, threw her flannel pajamas in a small bag and headed toward Boonetown.

Avery was in the yard putting a couple of wrapped Christmas presents in the truck. He looked up when he saw Maggie pull in the driveway. He closed the truck door and came over to the car. "I was wondering when you were going to get here."

"Yeah, I sort of took my time this morning. Do you think it's going to snow?"

"Nah, just going to mist and spit. We haven't had a big'n in near about ten years," said Avery. "Be nice to see a little snow. It would kill the bugs and help the crops next spring."

"What're you doing with those presents?"

"I bought the boys over at the slaughterhouse some Kentucky Bourbon for Christmas. They always do a bang-up job on the calf for us. It never hurts to let people know you appreciate them. Do you want to go with me? Your mama's at her sister's house. We can be back before she's back."

"Sure, I love riding around in this old truck. It reminds me of when I was a little girl and you let me set on your lap and drive," said Maggie, laughing.

"I reckon those were the good ole days. But, there're still good times. They're just different," said Avery.

Avery and Maggie were comfortable in the ole truck. It had been their 'talking place' longer than either of them could remember. There was just something about the cab of a truck—close and personal. It wasn't really snowing, like Avery said, just misting and spitting. The heater was warm. Maggie curled up on the passenger side and peered out the window. She didn't even bring her coat. Avery was driving a little faster than normal. The Slaughterhouse closed at one on Saturday. The grass was beginning to turn white—just a dusting, but it was turning colder as they moved to higher elevations.

"Ooooooooooo, no!" screamed Avery as he threw on the breaks and swerved to miss a raccoon that lumbered across the road. The truck spun sideways and slide into a muddy embankment. Avery cut the motor and got out of the truck to check the damage. He went skidding across the road bringing him to his knees.

"I'll be dern if there's not ice on the road," said Avery.

"That's all we need is to have the truck in a ditch," said Maggie. "I hope this doesn't make us late."

"Let me see if we can pull her out," said Avery. Maggie slid out of the truck into the mud and Avery tried to free the truck. The back wheels spun deeper into the mud and snow. "No, she ain't moving, we need help," said Avery. "Martha and George Anderson live about a fourth of a mile up the road."

"I remember hearing you talk about them. Don't they have a daughter?"

"Yeah, she's a good bit older than you. She went to a different school. She's been gone from here for over ten years," said Avery.

Although it was a short distance walking was tough. Most of it was up hill and some of it was slick. When Avery and Maggie entered the Anderson yard a pack of dogs greeted them. Avery called Sophie by name, patting her on the head. George came to the door. "I didn't hear no truck drive in, where did you come from?" asked George.

"We slipped off the road a ways back. I was wondering if you could take the tractor and pull us out of the ditch," said Avery. "I was trying to miss a coon," laughing.

"Any other time you'd be trying to hit him," said George, sharing the laugh.

"Have you taken ole Red out hunting anymore?"

"Yeah, that fellow from Durant came up last week and we went, but he really needs to go with Banjo to get the training." Avery looked around at the sorry lot of dogs and thought, *you've got that right. Banjo is the best dog around and come spring at the time trials I'll prove it.*

Maggie was standing to the side just listening. She started to follow George and Avery to the barn when Avery turned and said, "Maggie, you stay here with Martha while we go get the truck out of the ditch,"

George came back and stuck his head in the front door. "Hey, Martha come out here and meet Avery's girl." Martha came out looking a little puzzled.

"Hi, I'm Maggie."

Martha gripped Maggie's hand. "Come on in. It ain't much, but it's warm in here." The room was dark and unkempt. Maggie could tell Martha had not been out of bed long. The fireplace was a welcome sight. Maggie's black hair was wet from the falling snow and her hands were like ice. Martha reached out to touch Maggie's hair, but pulled her hand back. "You look so much like. . . .," said Martha, stopping in midsentence.

"I look so much like?" asked Maggie.

"Never mind, I was just thinking," said Martha. "Would you like a cup of hot chocolate?"

"That sounds wonderful. Did you expect this kind of weather today?" asked Maggie.

"No, I don't listen to the news," said Martha.

While Maggie and Martha sat in front of the fireplace drinking their hot chocolate, George and Avery headed down the road on the tractor to pull the truck out of the ditch.

George hooked a chain around the front of the truck chassis and easily pulled the truck out of the ditch. Avery followed behind George as they drove back to the house.

"Avery, you and George want some hot chocolate?" asked Martha.

"Oh, no. I'd love to but we've got to hurry now to make it to the slaughterhouse before they close, and Lucy will be in a snit, wondering where we are. Maggie, you ready to go?" said Avery.

Maggie turned toward Martha, "Thank you for the hot chocolate and for letting me hang out. It sure was nice to get in out of the cold."

"You're welcome, any time," said Martha, as Avery and Maggie climbed into the ole muddy truck and headed down the hill to the slaughterhouse.

"Martha seems sad," said Maggie.

"George is barely making it. Their daughter is missing," said Avery.

"That's odd. She's the second person I've heard of in the last month who has gone missing," said Maggie. "Who's looking for her?"

"Her husband has hired some government people and the sheriff is doing his best," said Avery. "The world can be a mighty mean place. I worry about you living by yourself and being out at night. Be careful." Avery turned his head toward the window and swallowed hard.

"I'm always careful. My daddy taught me to always be on the lookout," winking at Avery with a cocky smile. "I almost forgot to tell you. . . I have a new student. Her name is Mary Alice. She is so sweet. As a matter of fact, she reminds me of me when I was her age. Do we still have that first-grade picture of me in the stripped polo shirt and bibbed overalls? I would love to put our pictures side by side," said Maggie.

"That picture is in the dresser drawer. I saw it the other day. You were a cocky little girl," said Avery.

"Her daddy works at The Farm. I told him about Junior and he's going to see if he can locate him. He said he would let us know how Junior is getting along," said Maggie.

"That's great. I was talking to Joe last week and he's really worried," said Avery, as they pulled into the slaughterhouse parking lot. Jim and another fellow were standing near their cars.

"Hello, Mr. Sutton," said Jim. "Can I help you with something?"

"Yeah, you can take these Christmas presents inside for me. It's not much. Just a little something to say 'thank you' for your good work," said Avery.

"Sure thing," said Jim, as he took the presents from Avery.

When Avery and Maggie arrived home, Lucy was standing in the front door. "I've been worried sick-snow coming down and getting colder by the minute.

"You weren't here and I wanted to get those Christmas presents over to the boys before the weather turned bad. Maggie showed up just as I was leaving and she decided to go with me. We're back, now. Calm down. What's for supper?" said Avery.

"All you think about is eating. Come on in Maggie. You can help me whip up something."

"How've you been?" asked Maggie, giving her mother a little hug.

"I've been better, but I reckon I'll live," said Lucy, as she and Maggie headed for the kitchen to make supper.

It was a quiet night, snow silently falling, blanketing the ground and fence posts in creamy white frosting. There was something about the morning sun kissing the snowdrifts that beckoned Maggie to get outside and make snow angels, but she squelched the desire. She wanted her parents to see her as a responsible adult, not the child they had raised. She found herself thinking about Mary Alice. *If I had a little girl, we could make snow angels and no one would have to know how much fun I was having. They would just think I was doing it for my child. Maybe that's why I love teaching so much. I can play no matter who is watching. I wonder if I'll ever have a child of my own?*

Lucy called 'breakfast' and Maggie pulled on her sweats and hurried to the kitchen. The ham and biscuit breakfast was everything Maggie had dreamed about. Lucy made great red-eye gravy. "Can I take a couple of biscuits and two pieces of ham for my breakfast tomorrow?" asked Maggie.

"You know you can, but don't eat too much and make yourself sick," said Lucy.

"I need to leave in about an hour. I have papers to grade and I want to prepare for next week's reading groups. My new little girl is so smart. I'm having to find extra things for her to do. I also want to go to the library and check out some books that will challenge her reading skills," said Maggie.

"If you ask me, you're working far too hard for the money they pay you. They don't expect you to do all that extra work, do they?" said Lucy.

"I could get by with less work, but my kids are important to me. I want to do the best I can for them. They're my joy," said Maggie.

"Have it your way. It's your funeral," said Lucy, as Maggie left for Durant.

Chapter 5

Christmas was closing in fast. It was only eight days until Christmas holidays. Maggie would have two weeks off. Most of the children had finished their semester with ease and were at least reading at grade-level. Mary Alice had excelled in every subject. Maggie thought of advancing her early but did not want to see her go. She had quickly become Maggie's favorite student. *Is it because she doesn't have a mother at home? No, it's more than that.* Maggie tried to understand why she felt so close to Mary Alice. It was a mystery; a feeling Maggie couldn't explain.

The children helped Maggie hang ornaments on a small Christmas tree. The boys were running and talking. The girls giggled as they placed ribbons on the tree. They drew names and Maggie bought yoyos and filled a stocking with candy and fruit for everyone. She told the children their presents should not cost more than a dollar and if they didn't have a dollar to let her know. Two of the children asked for help and Maggie gladly helped, keeping their need confidential. The Christmas party made everyone smile, even Mary Alice. Several mothers brought cookies and Maggie made punch. The children exchanged presents and Maggie had a desk full of gifts. She treasured every child and every expression of their love for her.

"Mary Alice didn't tell me I needed to bring cookies," said Brian Scott.

"Oh, no, you didn't need to bring cookies," said Maggie. "We had plenty. Several of the mothers baked and I made punch. The children didn't need to eat any more sugar."

"I'm going to take Mary Alice to Missouri to be with my parents for Christmas. I'll come back to The Farm and work over the holidays except for Christmas Eve and Christmas Day. I found Junior Joseph. He said he wouldn't mind a visit from you. Would you like to take a tour of The Farm and meet J. J.?

"I think that's a great idea. When I go home for Christmas, I can fill Daddy in on his condition," said Maggie.

"I'll take Mary Alice to Missouri this week-end and have next week free. Which day will be best for you?" asked Brian Scott.

"How about Wednesday?" said Maggie, thinking by midweek she would have time to shop for her parents before Christmas on Saturday.

"Wednesday it is. I'll call you with the information," said Brian Scott.

Maggie shopped almost all day on Monday. It was hard to buy for her parents. They had everything they needed. She ended up with a red sweater for her mother, a pair of coveralls for her daddy and a box of candy and socks to give to Junior. She also bought Christmas candy and fruit for her parents. They didn't put up a tree or stockings. Christmas was low key at their house. Lucy said she only got fruit when she was a child and Avery said he rarely got anything. However, he did hear about how he was a Christmas surprise. His uncle Joe who loved to taunt and keep things stirred up told him his mother didn't want another baby. She wouldn't let his daddy touch her until his daddy bought her a beautiful dress and hat for Christmas. "She forgot to be distant and here you came," laughed Joe. "You only weighed four pounds. They didn't think you'd live and your mama was glad, but your daddy saw to you and got what you needed and you made it." Maggie had heard that story most of her life and was thankful for her grandfather. He was a kind man, but Avery often said his mother was mean.

Brian Scott called on Tuesday night. "What if I pick you up around 10:00 a.m.? It'll take us about twenty minutes to drive out to The Farm. J. J. is expecting us and his supervisor is aware he'll have visitors around ten-thirty. He'll meet us in the visitor's lounge."

"That sounds like a plan," said Maggie. "I'll be waiting. Do you have my address?"

He did have Maggie's address, but he didn't want her to know he had investigated her. "What is it?" he asked.

"Twenty-seven hundred, Main Street. You know Durant," said Maggie.

"Great, I'll see you tomorrow," said Mr. Scott.

Brian arrived on time in his shiny new maroon Lincoln. Maggie was waiting on the front porch. Looking up from her thoughts she immediately went to the car. "Good morning," she said. "This is some fancy car you have here," as she climbed in on the passenger side.

"Yeah, it's a special issue, has a lot of amenities, plus 'get away' power," said Brian, smiling.

"Mr. Scott, is this a telephone? I didn't know you could have a phone in a car." said Maggie.

"Yes, it's possible now in some business vehicles," said Brian. "Since we're becoming friends, do you think we can dispense with the Mister and just call me Brian? We are becoming friends, aren't we?"

"Yes, of course and you can call me Maggie, except when we're around the kids and then I'm Ms. Maggie."

"I understand, so Maggie it is," said Brian, as they pulled into the parking lot at The Farm.

"I can't believe how big this place is," said Maggie. "How long have you worked here?"

"I've only been attached to this station for about three months," said Brian.

"What do you do here?"

"If I tell you that, I'll have to kill you," said Brian, laughing.

"I guess I'll just have to get used to being in the dark," said Maggie.

"It's best. What you don't know can't hurt you," said Brian, as he opened the door to enter the building. Just past the receptionist there were huge locked doors.

"Good morning," said the receptionist.

"Good morning, we're here to see Junior Joseph. I believe he's on your schedule?"

"Yes, I'll have the orderly bring him to the visitor's room. It'll only take a minute."

"We'll go on back," said Brian, motioning to Maggie. "Buzz us in." The receptionist complied and the big heavy doors opened. Brian and Maggie entered the visitor's room to find a young black man sitting on the couch. He rose when they entered. "Hello," said Brian. "This is Maggie Adams. I believe you know her daddy?"

"Mr. Avery and my daddy were raised in the same house," said Junior. I've seen Mr. Avery on and off, but I never had the pleasure of meeting Ms. Maggie."

"Please, just call me Maggie. I understand they call you J. J. here. Would you rather be called Junior or J. J.?"

"Junior is fine. Daddy said it was after Mr. Junior Sutton. That would have been your great granddaddy. My daddy loves your family. They were his family for a long time."

"Time changes everything. It's too bad Daddy and your daddy didn't stay close," said Maggie. "Well, how have you been? Your daddy is worried about you. That's the reason I'm here. I live in Durant and it was easier for me to come than Daddy. How much longer before you'll be released?"

"I could have been released before now, but I volunteered to help with some experiments," said Junior.

"So that means you're here of your own volition?" said Maggie.

"Yeah, I guess that's what it means. It's confusing sometimes. I think I'm off the stuff and then I'm not. I'm not exactly sure how to think about it," said Junior.

Maggie sat down on the couch beside Junior, placing her package on the floor. Brian was standing near the door, observing. "Oh, I brought you something," said Maggie. "It's not much but I wanted to say Merry Christmas," handing the sack to Junior.

"Thank you. You really didn't have to do this. We have everything we need here," said Junior.

"I know, but Merry Christmas, anyway," said Maggie, as Junior pulled his socks out of the bag.

"A body can always use more socks," said Junior.

"Our time is running short," said Brian. "Is there a message you'd like to send to your daddy?"

"Tell him I'm doing alright and I'll be home soon," said Junior.

Chapter 6

After a short tour, Maggie and Brian left the compound headed toward town. "It's lunch time. Are you hungry?" asked Brian. "There's a great meat and three between here and your house, how about we stop and get a bite. I really hate eating alone."

"As a matter of fact, I am hungry. I'll pay since you were so nice to arrange my visit with Junior," said Maggie.

"Gratuity accepted," said Brian, smiling.

Maggie and Brian entered the restaurant and grabbed a corner table. The place was busy indicating good food and hospitality. "Look, they have pot roast. I love a good beef roast," said Brian.

"I'll have chicken," said Maggie. "I have a freezer full of beef. You haven't eaten beef until you eat beef my daddy corn feeds. He gives me half a calf every year. I'll have to make you a roast sometime."

"Sounds like a novel idea. If you're still willing, maybe when Mary Alice is back, we can take some roast beef sandwiches to the park," said Brian.

"How long will she be in Missouri?" asked Maggie.

"I hope just until the holidays are over," said Brian. "We'd better get going. I still have Christmas shopping to do."

"Thank God, I'm finished. I've just got to wrap," said Maggie as they left the restaurant.

Stan knew he would buy Jamie a bicycle, but his parents were another matter. Last year he had purchased his parents a trash compactor and his daddy threw a fit. He wasn't going to have some kind of new-fangled 'trash fixer' in his house. He had been taking care of the trash for thirty years and he knew how to do it. Truth is, he threw it in the big sink hole back of the barn. Stan knew what was happening. The trash was ending up eventually in the water supply. But there was no consoling his dad. He was not having that contraption in his house and that settled it. Stan took the compactor home where he and Jenny had the privilege of compacting their trash. Stan decided he would just give them money and a nice card; yes, $100 each would make them smile.

The trip seemed long, but Stan finally arrived in Missouri where the Christmas tree was up and decorated. "Look," said Jamie, "I helped decorate the tree. See the angel. He's watching over baby Jesus and grandma says he watches over me, too."

"That's beautiful," said Stan. "Grandma and the angel will keep you safe. Do you feel safe here?"

"I feel good here, but do I have to be Mary Alice here?"

"No, me, Grandma and Grandpa can call you Jamie if we don't say it too loud," said Stan, grabbing Jamie and tickling her.

"How's the investigation going?" asked Mrs. Turner. "You would think with all the influence you have you would have turned up something by now."

"Mama, we're getting close. That's all I can tell you," said Stan. "I've never seen so many gifts. Who're they for?"

"Most are for Jamie. There may be one or two in there for you," said Stan's mom.

Christmas morning was fun. Santa Clause brought the bicycle and money. Stan's daddy said he didn't know Santa gave out hundred-dollar bills. He would have to be nicer to him next time he saw him at the department store. Brian received a new shirt and socks. His mother cooked a huge dinner with five desserts. She said Stan and Jamie would have to take the cake and candy home with them. Neither of them objected. Stan could share the sweets with his friends at The Farm and with Maggie if Jamie asked to see her again before school started back. "Jamie is out of school for another week. I'll pick her up next week-end," said Stan and he left for Durant.

On the way home, Stan stopped and picked up a large fruit basket. He couldn't imagine how Jenny's parents were feeling this Christmas. He kept driving until he reached their house. Pulling into the yard, the dogs met him with loud yelps. George and Martha came to the door.

"Hey, there," said George. "I wasn't sure we'd see you this Christmas."

"I wasn't sure I would get to come, but I'm here. I'm sorry Jamie's not with me. I left her at my parent's house. She's safer there. I'm not exactly sure what has happened to Jenny, but I'm sure it's foul play. We all know she just wouldn't up and leave and the investigation is coming along. I know this can't be a Merry Christmas, but I brought you some fruit and candy," said Stan.

"Come in and get out of the cold. Martha made a fruit cake and coffee," said George. "We were just fixing to tear into it."

"That sounds good," said Stan, as they sat silently by the fire.

"Martha, where's that cake?" asked George.

Martha brought the cake and poured three cups of coffee. She put a dab of milk in her cup, as she joined the men by the fire.

Finally speaking, "I've been working on Jamie's present for about six months, said George. "I've made her a dollhouse. It even has electricity. Martha made little curtains and bed coverings. I've carved some furniture for it. Martha framed a small picture of Jamie and we put it on the wall. The lights are battery operated. We've had a good time making it for her," as he went to the spare room to retrieve the gift. He brought the dollhouse and sat it down in front of Stan.

"This is remarkable," said Stan, examining the dollhouse. "You have a real talent." The little house was a two-bedroom A-frame with flashlight bulbs in the ceiling for lights. The tiny bed had a real quilt on it and the kitchen had a sink, stove and a round oak table with two small straight-back chairs. There was no bathroom, but George and Martha didn't have a bathroom either. The 'outhouse' was still in use. The spare bedroom was empty. "The spare room will give me something to work on for Jamie's birthday," said George. "It's almost easier to carve a big piece of furniture than this little tiny stuff."

"Jamie received a set of little people from my parents. They should be the perfect family to live in their new house," said Stan. "Jamie will be over the moon."

George sat the dollhouse by the front door and came back to the fire. "So, do you think you'll find our girl anytime soon?" he asked.

"To be honest, I think something has happened to her. I believe we'll find her, but I don't know how it will turn out," said Stan.

Martha was listening from the kitchen where she was cleaning up the dishes. Stan could hear her crying.

"What's been happening around here?" asked Stan.

"Not much, that fellow from Durant has been up a couple of times to go hunting. He's Avery Sutton's friend. That redbone hound he gave me is learning how to hunt. I guess I'll enter him in the trials in May.

"Anybody else been around?" asked Stan.

"Well, yes, that Pentecostal pastor, Robby, from Boonetown came. They seem like odd bedfellows if you ask me, but I guess coon hunting brings all kinds together," said George.

Stan's thoughts were going wild. There was another link to Boonetown. It was close to 8:00 p.m. and he knew Martha and George usually went to bed before nine. "I'd best be going," said Stan. "I have a way to go and I'm already tired."

"Thanks for remembering us," said Martha. "Bring Jamie when you can. We'd love to see her."

"I will. She wants to see you, too," said Stan as he hurried out the door. He was half-way to Durant before he realized he had left the dollhouse behind.

It was already late, but Stan knew he had to go back to Pilot Ridge. He had left the dollhouse behind and he wanted to have it to give to Jamie when he brought her home. He picked up his phone and rang George and Martha's number. "Hello, this is Stan. Well, you know I walked right out and left the dollhouse."

"Oh, did you leave it? We haven't noticed. We really wanted Jamie to have it for Christmas," said George.

"It's eight-thirty. I'll try to be there by nine-thirty, ten at the latest. I want to have it for her when I pick her up tomorrow," said Stan.

"Don't bother about us. We'll stay up and wait for you," said George.

Stan had turned around and headed back when the car phone rang. "This is Sheriff Madden from Boonetown. I wanted you to be the first to know. We've found a body. It may be Jenny, looks like she has been in Salt Creek for a while. She'll be hard to identify. I'll go up to Martha and George's place in the morning and tell them. It might not hurt if you were there with them," said the Sheriff.

"I was just headed that way. I'll try and get them to let me spend the night, without telling them why," said Stan.

"I'll meet you there in the morning," said the Sheriff.

Stan hung up the phone, numb. He knew this would happen, but now that it had, he was in shock, operating off rote. Right now, he had to concentrate on driving to Pilot Ridge. *It's possible, it could be someone else.* He knew better than jump to conclusions. He would wait to see the evidence.

Sure enough, Martha and George were up, porch light on, waiting for Stan. They were excited that Jamie would get her Christmas present on time. "Come on in here, I'm sorry you had to come all this way back. I should have reminded you to take the dollhouse, but my mind is a mess now-days," said George.

"I know how you feel. I'm not in very good shape myself. I'm tired. Seems like everything is coming down at once," said Stan. "It's a long way back home and I dread driving it."

"You don't need to be driving this late at night, tired and all. You should just spend the night and drive back in the morning," said Martha.

"That's not a bad idea," said Stan. But, first let me put the dollhouse in the car. I don't want to forget it again."

"The spare room is made up. You should be comfortable in there. If you get cold there's an extra quilt on the chair," said Martha.

"Thank you," said Stan, as he closed the door and took his clothes off down to his underwear. That's how he slept at home. He reached for the quilt. The night seemed extra cold. He would take any comfort that came his way. He was tired but couldn't sleep. His body was tense. When he did sleep, dark dreams interrupted his rest. He pulled the quilt over his head and finally slept.

Stan heard George and Martha up at six but stayed in bed until Martha called "Breakfast". She had gone all out to make him a big breakfast. He dressed fast and went to the table. It was all he could do to force his food down. He sipped his coffee wondering what time the sheriff would arrive. All the while Martha was saying, "Take out some more gravy for that biscuit. You don't eat enough to keep a bird alive."

"Oh, I eat enough," said Stan. I'm beginning to get a belly on me," pooching his belly out.

"That ain't no belly. You ought to see George with his shirt off. Now that's a belly," said Martha, laughing.

"Just shows a man enjoys his dinner," said George, smiling.

A car pulled into the yard. The dogs came around the house in a mad rush, barking like they'd eat you up. "Hey, Sophie, good dog," said Shariff Madden, patting her on the head. George, Martha and Stan went to the front door.

"It's the sheriff," said George, turning, looking back at Martha and Stan. "Good Morning, Sheriff," said George. What brings you our way?"

"I've got some news. Can I come in?"

"Sure, come in and sit down. Can I get you some coffee?"

"No thank you, I need to tell all of you something. Some hunters found the body of a woman in Salt Creek. It's pretty decomposed. I can't swear it's Jenny, but it may be," said the sheriff. "They're taking the body to the county coroner's office in Durant. I'll need all three of you to come down there tomorrow around 10:00 a.m. to see if you can identify the body."

Martha was shaking her head and crying. "Lord don't let it be my baby," she said. Stan went over and put his arm around her.

"We hope it's not, but she has been missing for a long time now. Don't cross any bridges till you get there. We'll hope for the best," said Stan, as he headed for the door. "I had better get back to Durant and see if I can find out anything else. I'll see you at the coroner at 10:00 o'clock tomorrow. George, do you know how to get there?"

"Yes," said George. "I had to help identify another person once."

"Be careful driving down," said Stan, as he gave Martha a little hug and hurried back to Durant.

The next morning George was sitting on the porch waiting for Martha to finish dressing, wondering how Stan was holding up and if he made it back to Durant. Turning his head slightly he glimpsed Avery coming alongside the porch. The dogs knew Avery so well they didn't even bark. "Avery is that you?" asked George, squinting. "I didn't hear you drive in."

"I'm quiet, this morning," said Avery, grinning. "What you doing all dressed up sitting out here on your porch? You going somewhere?"

"I'm waiting on Martha. Some hunters found a woman's body in Salt Creek. They think it might be Jenny. They want us to come to see if we can identify her this morning."

Avery turned pale as he pulled a chair up and sat down, "Would it be alright if an old friend goes with you and Martha? It must be hard on you," said Avery.

"I'd like that. You've known Jenny since she was a baby. Your opinion and advice will be greatly appreciated. The sheriff said it won't be a pretty sight. I tried to get Martha to stay home, but she insisted on going. Says that's the least she can do for her daughter."

Martha hurried out the front door dressed in her Sunday black dress complete with veiled hat and white gloves.

"Morning Martha," said Avery.

"Morning, Avery, what're you doing here?"

"I came about some fool dog, but George told me about the woman found in Salt Creek and now I've forgot about the dog," said Avery. "I'm going with you to Durant."

All three piled into George's old grey Ford truck and headed to Durant. Words failed them. The cab was quiet as they rumbled along plunged deep in their own thoughts and prayers.

"Come in," said Sheriff Madden. "We'll be with you directly."

Stan was already waiting. He rose when the Andersons and Avery entered. George reached over and shook his hand. "Have you met my friend, Avery Sutton? Avery, this is my son-in-law."

"Nice to meet you," said Avery. "I'm sorry it's under these circumstances."

The receptionist interrupted. "Anderson family," she called.

"Yes, that's us," said George. "They called us, patting Martha on the hand, bringing her out of her trance.

The morgue was cold—stainless steel drawers lined the wall. The attendant said, "brace yourself, it's bad," as he pulled the drawer open. Martha gasped, falling to the floor. George and Avery lifted her up and sat her on a nearby chair. Stan, George and Avery stepped forward to get a better look. "That's her hand, I gave her that ring," said Stan. "The bastard didn't even take her jewelry. She always wore green nail polish. There's still some on her left thumb. She loved green."

"Her face is pretty messed up. I'm not sure it's her," said George. Avery stood still peering down at her cold mangled body.

"There's a new test called, DNA," said Stan. "It's not being used yet by the general public, and it's still in developmental stages, but it could help us identify her. I think I can get it done at the department."

"How does it work?" asked George.

"I'll take a sample of your hair and we can compare it to a sample of this woman's hair and the lab can look at the two hairs together and see if the deoxyribonucleic acid helix matches," said Stan. If they match, she's your daughter, if not she's another unfortunate woman.

"No," said Martha and Avery almost together. "It doesn't seem right," said Martha.

"It doesn't hurt anyone," said Stan. "As a matter of fact, Martha you can give me a hair and we'll take a hair off the corpse and I'll do the rest.

"If you're sure," said Martha, looking relieved.

Stan took the samples and told the sheriff he would be in touch. The case was not under Stan's jurisdiction, but Shariff Madden knew Stan and trusted his knowledge and expertise.

Martha, Avery and George drove back to Pilot Ridge without talking.

The Farm

Stan had three more days before picking up Jamie. He checked in with Junior. Things were going well. His parole hearing was set in two weeks. Stan logged the date in on his calendar. He wanted to make sure he was there to put in a good word for Junior. He had visited with Junior often. The summer session at the law enforcement academy would start in May. Stan thought Junior would make a good CIA agent. He approached Junior with the idea. He wanted to make sure Junior was ready. Stan had already ordered enrollment papers and with his recommendation he was sure Junior would be accepted. The school was just outside Durant. The last two months required Junior to be present day and night on campus. Stan was toying with the idea of inviting Junior to live with him during the first four months.

"When you work for the CIA you're on duty twenty-four-seven. Your total loyalty is required. That's the reason it's good you're not married; nothing can get in the way of you doing your job. I've let my marriage hinder me and now my wife is missing," said Stan.

"I appreciate the confidence you have in me. I'm sorry about your wife. I'm beginning to understand how dangerous your job is. I wish I could help. I know it must be hard on you," said Junior.

"If you accept our offer, you'll be ready to help soon. I'm looking forward to working with you," said Stan, as he left the visitor's room to go back to his office.

Jeff Newman stuck his head in the door. "How are you holding up?" he asked.

"I'm accustomed to dealing with hard things. I'm trying to take it one step at a time and keep a level head, but when it's your wife that's missing. . ."

"Did your latest trip to Mexico help with the drug investigation?" asked Jeff.

"Bits and pieces," said Stan. "Not enough to go to court."

"Well, you know I'm always here if you need to talk and we do have a professional Psychiatrist on staff. It can't be easy. You may need to take yourself off the case," said Jeff.

"There's no evidence that Jenny is tied to the drug case," said Stan. "J. Morris is handling Jenny's case, which reminds me, I need to talk to him. Thanks, I know you'll be here if I need you."

Stan had mailed the hair samples to a lab in Washington D.C. It would take about two weeks to get the results. Junior was waiting for him in the visitor's room. "How was Christmas?" asked Stan.

"It was alright. I went to the festival. The music was good. I also went to a church service. God did a good thing when He came to earth. It made me want to do better. I don't want to be on drugs, and I will get clean," said Junior.

"I did some investigating and found out they have been drying you out and then giving you heroin to make you addicted again so they can try another drug to get you off again. I don't think you understood what they were going to do. Once you're clean, I suggest you withdraw your volunteer request. It'll be difficult to stay clean, but I believe you can do it," said Stan.

"Really? I've noticed some of the other fellows experiencing the same kind of cycles. I thought they were giving me medication," said Junior. "I guess I didn't understand."

"Well, if you call heroin medication," said Stan.

"I'll see about getting out of the volunteer program. I know it won't be easy," said Junior.

"It won't be easy when you go home either," said Stan. "Your old druggy friends and the guy that sold you the drugs in the first place will be bound to approach you. What kind of work did you do before you were arrested?"

"There's not much opportunity for a black man in Boonetown. I farmed with Daddy and did odd jobs. I'm not a bad carpenter," said Junior. "I finished high school at the top of my class. I'm not dumb. I reckon I could do just about anything with some instruction."

"Have you decided to accept our offer? There's a scholarship program. It'll take about six months. Maybe together we can do something about the drug problem in Durant. Having been through it you'll be better equipped to help others."

"Why me?"

"Because I see a lot of potential in you and we need people like you—someone who is determined and I admit because you're a black man you'll have an advantage to bringing down some of the pushers. Many of them are black. I don't know where you purchased your first drugs, but I believe someday you'll trust me enough to tell me, said Stan.

"I don't want to get anybody in trouble," said Junior.

"Think of the lives they're destroying," said Stan. "They probably don't even realize what they're doing."

"You make a mighty good argument. I never dreamed of having an important career. I still need to think about it," said Junior.

"You'll train at the CIA Crime and Narcotics Center in Durant. Actually, you can crash at my place while you're in school. Remember anything you tell me will remain between us. There're a lot of secrets in this business," said Stan. "As a matter of fact, I'm under the alias of Brian Scott when away from The Farm. I may be John Doe the next time we talk."

In two days, Stan and Junior met again. Junior had withdrawn from the volunteer drug program and told Stan he was ready to accept the offer to attend the Law Enforcement Academy.

"Junior, I want to make sure you understand, you may not tell anyone about joining the CIA or about my undercover work, not even your daddy," said Stan. "Do you understand?"

"Well, yes, I guess so," said Junior. "I told Maggie about me going into law enforcement. She has been to see me several times."

"Are you and Maggie thinking of dating?" asked Stan.

"She's a really beautiful girl. I've thought about asking her out," said Junior.

"It seems like you're getting close," said Stan.

"I'm taking your advice seriously about not being involved with a woman. I want to be a good officer," said Junior. "Maggie and I are just good friends."

"Your first assignment will be maintenance at a government building. It won't be glamorous, and you must do a good job and never tell anyone why you're really there," said Stan. "Tell your daddy you got a job working for the government. If he asks what, say maintenance and leave it at that."

"I never was able to lie with a straight face," said Junior.

"You won't be lying. You'll be doing maintenance," said Stan.

Chapter 7

Stan brought Mary Alice back to Durant with more toys than he could carry. The dollhouse was still in the car. "Papa and Grandma Anderson made this for you," said Stan.

"I love it," said Jamie. "My little people will love it, too." She played with her dollhouse and little people all the way home, leaving Stan alone with his thoughts: *How can I ever explain Jenny's death to Jamie? She's a smart little girl, but what does she understand about death? I know she misses her mother. Maggie will help. Jamie trusts her.*

"Daddy, will Mommy be home when we get back," cut in Jamie.

"No, sweetheart I don't believe she will," said Stan.

"Can I take mommy's picture to school with me tomorrow?" asked Jamie.

"I wish you could, but I think it's best if you keep her picture at home," said Stan.

Jamie curled up on the back seat and began playing with her little people again. She had the daddy and the little girl in the bedroom together but took the mommy to the living room and laid her on the floor.

Monday morning school came with a new year-1959. Maggie was laughing because she had already put the wrong date on three checks. It always took her a while to adjust, so the first thing she did when she arrived in her classroom was change the year on the calendar. At least her children would know what year it was.

Mary Alice and Brian arrived on time. Maggie was standing at the door greeting her students. "Good morning, happy new year," said Maggie as they entered.

Mary Alice ran over to Paula by the book corner. "Hi," she said. "Which book are you reading?"

"*The Happy Family*," said Paula.

"Does your mommy live at your home?" asked Mary Alice.

"Yes, and my daddy and my brother and my big sister," said Paula. "Who lives at your house?"

"I. . . I'm not sure," said Mary Alice.

Brian was still standing by the door waiting for Maggie to finish talking to another parent. "Can we talk in private?" he asked.

"Let me call for an aide," said Maggie. She punched the intercom button. "Yes, Ms. Maggie, what can I do for you?" said the secretary.

"Is there an assistant in the office? A parent has asked for a conference," said Maggie.

"Yes, she'll be right there," said the secretary.

"Anyone using the conference room?" asked Maggie.

"Nope, it's all yours," said the secretary.

"As soon as she gets here, I'll meet you in the conference room," said Maggie.

Brian left Maggie greeting the other children and their parents. When the aide arrived Maggie joined Brian and sat down across the table from him. "Now, what do we need to talk about?" she asked.

"Hunters found a woman's body in Salt Creek. It's most likely my wife. It's hard to tell. We've taken a test that will take about two weeks to get the results. I'm going to let Mary Alice stay in school if I can. I may have to take her out again in two weeks. She wanted to come back so bad. She has really missed you," said Brian. "If I have to take her back to Missouri, do you think you can prepare lessons for her and mail them to my mother? I'll give you a post office box number and pay the postage. If this is my wife's body, I don't know how in the world I'll ever talk to Mary Alice about her death."

"It will be hard. Let's hope it doesn't come to that, but if it does, I'll be glad to help," said Maggie. "I've got to get back to my class, but while we're at it, thanks for helping Junior. He told me you helped him get into law enforcement school. His daddy and my daddy are coming to pick him up next week when he's released."

"He'll make a good law enforcement officer," said Brian. "But nobody needs to know what he's doing. He shouldn't have told you."

"I know how to keep a secret," said Maggie.

"I'll let you know about Jenny as soon as I find out," said Brian. "Don't be talking about her to anyone. I only told you because of Mary Alice."

"I'll be waiting to hear and I'm sorry," said Maggie.

"Thank you, I'll be in touch," said Brian, as he left.

Trying to remain calm, Maggie returned to her classroom. "Did everyone have a great Christmas?" she asked. "Take out a clean piece of paper and your crayons. I want you to draw a picture of the best thing you did for Christmas," said Maggie.

Mary Alice drew a house with little people inside. The little man and the little girl were together, but the little woman was off to the side lying on the floor. Paula drew her family together with their hands in the air singing "Here Comes Santa Clause." She said they always sang songs at Christmas. Almost all the children drew family.

After the children talked about their Christmas pictures, Maggie said they could have a 'choose your activity' time. Mary Alice and Paula choose puzzles. Maggie sat at her desk observing. After finishing her puzzle, Mary Alice came to Maggie, whispering. "Can I tell you something?" she asked, putting her hand over her mouth next to Maggie's ear.

"Yes, of course," said Maggie.

"My name is not Mary Alice Scott," whispered Mary Alice. "My name is Jamie Leigh Turner. Don't tell Daddy I told you. He said we're playing a game where I have to be Mary Alice Scott."

"Your secret is safe with me," said Maggie. But I think we'd better continue calling you Mary Alice until your daddy says we can call you Jamie."

Frowning, "Ok," said Mary Alice and went back to the puzzle table.

Chapter 8

Avery hurried to pick Joe up at his little farm just outside Boonetown. He was proud of his new silver Chevy truck. "Whew, when did you get this new truck?" asked Joe.

"I've had it three or four days, I guess," said Avery.

"I've never made enough money to even buy a used truck, much less a brand new one," said Joe.

"I figure a new truck every twenty years ain't bad," laughed Avery. But I tell you what."

"What's that," asked Joe.

"Junior drives, doesn't he? When we get back, we'll run by the house and get my ole red truck. I'm going to give it to you," said Avery. "And if you want him, I'll give you that blue-tic coonhound. I need to concentrate on Banjo until after the trials. The boys from Durant are coming up tomorrow night to take our dogs out again. They've got so they come almost every Friday night."

"I ain't much of a coon hunter, but it would be right fun to have a dog. My wife, Candy, won't care. I'll take real good care of the truck and Junior will love having a way to go when he's here. You know he's doing really good. I'm proud of him," said Joe.

"Maggie tells me she and Junior have become good friends. I don't see anything wrong with mixed couples, but racial tension is high right now. I don't know what the world would do if they were involved. And you know as well as I do, we can't let that happen for other reasons. It may be time to reveal our secret," said Avery.

"I've never told anyone. If we tell, then it'll be up to Maggie and Junior to keep the secret," said Joe.

"Or to tell it," said Avery. "I know Maggie. She just might be brazened enough to shout it to the world."

"It's been a long time, but times haven't changed much," said Joe. "Maybe we should tell them. Today, we can tell Junior we have a secret that we've shared for over thirty years and we need to pass it on to him and Maggie. We'll get together with Maggie the next time she comes to Boonetown. How does that sound?"

"Sounds alright," said Avery, as he pulled into the parking lot at The Farm. The receptionist told them Junior was just finishing up saying good-bye to his friends. They had given him a good-bye party with cake and ice cream. "He'll be out, directly," she said.

Junior came out smiling. "It's so good to see you," he said, hugging Joe. "Good morning Mr. Avery."

"Son, you're looking good," said Joe.

"I'm feeling good," said Junior, as they made their way to the truck. "Well, somebody has a new truck! Does Maggie know?"

"I haven't told her yet. She'll probably fuss and say she wants to keep riding in the ole red truck because she has so many memories. She can't remember us having any other vehicle," said Avery. "I just told your daddy; I'm giving the two of you the ole red truck."

Junior was speechless. "You are a true friend. That's where Maggie gets her generous spirit. She has really helped me. You know it's because of her I've got my new job. Her friend is helping me with training and after that I'll go to work for the government. I'll be doing maintenance in a government building in Durant."

"When will you start," asked Joe, stretching out his legs in the roomy new truck cab.

"It'll be about another month before I move to Durant. We'll have plenty of time to catch up," said Junior.

"When Maggie comes up to visit, the four of us need to get together," said Avery. "Joe and I have something we want to share with the both of you. I'll phone you and let you know when she's coming."

"She already told me she's coming next week-end. We had planned to get together and have lunch at the drugstore," said Junior.

"Junior, you know better than that. You might buy something at the drug store, but there's no way they'll let you sit down and talk to a white woman and have something to eat," said Joe.

"I guess you're right, but things are about to change," said Junior.

"Wishful thinking, if you ask me," said Joe.

"I'll talk to Maggie and we'll figure out something," said Junior.

Avery pulled his new truck up beside the ole red one. "Here we are, boys. Here's your truck. I even washed it for you."

'It's beautiful, clean or dirty," said Joe. "I don't know how to thank you."

"You've thanked me by being my friend from the time we were kids," said Avery. "If it weren't for you, I probably would be an invalid. You helped me learn to walk again. It's the least I can do for you."

Avery pitched the keys to Junior, as Junior got in the ole red truck. "Don't drive her too fast, now. She's old," said Avery, as Junior and Joe drove off in the direction of Boonetown.

The Farm

Stan made a point of going by his office before picking Jamie up from school. He was looking for a letter from the lab in Washington D.C. There was a stack of mail. The letter was on the bottom. He stood with it in his hand for a minute trying to take in the reality. This test would give him the information he needed to declare the corpse his wife or not. He ripped opened the letter:

January 10, 1960

Dear Mr. Turner.

The two sample hairs you sent us match indicating a close relationship between the two individuals. Stan laid the letter on his desk and sat down. *Jenny is dead,* he thought *and now it's up to me and J. Morris to find out who killed her.* He looked up at the clock. *It's almost three. I have to pick Jamie up from school. I can't be late. She has been through enough,* as he shut down his thoughts.

Before he left the office, he had to call Sheriff Madden. He turned off his thoughts and picked up the phone. The DNA matches," he said. "I'm ready to identify the corpse as my wife. Jenny wouldn't want us to draw this thing out too long."

"I agree," said Sheriff Madden. "We'll need to let her parents know."

"If her teacher can help me, we'll tell Jamie tomorrow. God, it's hard," said Stan, trying not to let the sheriff hear his pain.

"I know it's difficult. A man can think he's tough until his child is involved. That's the reason I think we both should be there when we tell George and Martha," said the sheriff.

"You're right. What about Sunday afternoon around two? I'll take Jamie back to Missouri to be with my parents tomorrow night," said Stan.

"I'll see you on Sunday," said the sheriff.

"Good day," said the receptionist. "Have a great week-end." Stan rushed pass her and out the door without responding. He was late. Jamie would be worried.

Chapter 9

Mary Alice was the last child to be picked up. She was waiting with Maggie holding her hand. "I assured her you were just running late," said Maggie.

"Daddy why are you so late?" asked Mary Alice.

"Daddy has had a rough day," said Brian. "Maggie, we need to talk. Can we have that roast beef sandwich day tomorrow at the park?"

"Yes, said Maggie, with understanding in her voice. "I'll make the roast tonight. You bring the chips and drinks. I heard the news earlier. It's supposed to be in the high sixties tomorrow. It should be nice."

"Mary Alice and I will pick you up at ten," said Brian. "There are picnic tables, bring a cloth of some kind to throw over the table in case the birds have gotten to it."

"Will do," said Maggie, giving Mary Alice a little hug. Maggie stayed in her room another hour straightening up and praying that she would have the wisdom Mary Alice needed to get through this time of grief. Maggie's heart ached for Brian. She took a soccer ball off the shelf to take with her to the park. Maybe they could kick it around some before they ate. But, after the roast beef it would be time to be serious, more serious than Maggie had ever been in her life.

Maggie put the roast in the crockpot. She was not looking forward to tomorrow. She went to bed early but found it hard to sleep. She lay in the bed thinking of Brian. Her heart hurt for him. His heartbreak brought back memories of Tom. She gave in to her feelings. It was good to cry. Sometimes it felt unreal to think about Tom being dead. It seemed like he was just away like he had been for most of their marriage.

Mary Alice and Brian arrived on time. Maggie was waiting. The sun was shining. Mary Alice was dressed warm, smiling, ready to have a wonderful day in the park with her daddy and her friend. She had no idea what was in her future, but Brian and Maggie were hurting inside and dreading what was coming next. If only they could spare Mary Alice this sorrow. No child should be put through losing her mother in such a brutal way.

"I brought the soccer ball," said Maggie. "Come play with me."

Brian grabbed the ball out of her hand, "I'll kick it over your head to Mary Alice. Get it, get it," yelled Brian, laughing. Mary Alice ran to get the ball and kicked it back, laughing, too. Maggie was glad she brought the ball. At least there was something fun about this day.

"It's twelve o'clock, I'm hungry," said Brian.

"Me too," said Maggie. "Hey, Mary Alice, are you hungry?"

"I don't think I like roast beef," said Mary Alice.

"Don't worry about that. I just happened to bring a peanut butter and jelly sandwich just for you," said Maggie.

"I like peanut butter and jelly," said Mary Alice.

"I've noticed," said Maggie.

"You're right this is the best roast beef I've ever eaten," said Brian, taking another big bite, as he opened his Coke. "Why didn't you tell me your daddy is Avery Sutton?"

"It never occurred to me. Why would my daddy's name be important to you?"

"I don't know. I actually met Mr. Sutton last week. You told me your daddy was coming with Junior's daddy and it just dawned on me when I saw Mr. Sutton and Junior's daddy leaving with Junior yesterday how we all seem to be connected in some way," said Brian.

Mary Alice came and sat on her daddy's knee. "I wish Mommy was here," she said. Brian looked at Maggie. His eyes said, "It's time." Maggie came and sat down by Brian.

"Honey, Daddy is so sorry, but Mommy won't be with us anymore. She went to heaven to live with God," said Brian.

"That's not fair. I want Mommy to live here with me," said Mary Alice.

"I wish she could, but she died," said Brian, batting back tears.

"Do you understand what it means to die?" asked Maggie.

"Not really," said Mary Alice.

"It's like your mommy had to move to a new house. "You've had to move a few times, haven't you?"

"Uh-hu," said Mary Alice, looking at the ground.

"We live in our bodies," said Maggie, touching Mary Alice's arm. "When God is ready for us to move to be with Him, He gives us a new body, like a new house. Your mommy didn't leave you on purpose. Her body, her house, got damaged and she couldn't live in it anymore, so God is taking care of her in heaven and giving her a new house to live in there." Maggie didn't know if she was making any sense or if Mary Alice was following her. "Do you understand?"

"Where's my mommy's old house," asked Mary Alice. Maggie looked at Brian.

"Her old body is at the coroner's lab," said Brian.

"What will happen to her old body?" asked Mary Alice.

"We'll have a good-bye party for her old body and celebrate the fact that she has a new body and that she's with God," said Brian.

"Can I go to the party?" asked Mary Alice.

"I think your mommy would like that," said Brian. He had not planned on taking Mary Alice, but now he felt like he had to. She wanted to be there and he had to let her say her last good-bye to her mother.

"While I'm making the arrangements for the party, I'll need to take you to Missouri again to stay with Papa and Grandma," said Brian.

"But I want to stay here with Ms. Maggie and you," said Mary Alice.

"I know and I'll bring you back as soon as I can," said Brian.

"Your daddy and I talked about it. While you're gone, each week, I'll send you a package with all of your assignments and new books to read and a love message from me because you know I love you, don't you? You'll be back before you know it and we'll go on another picnic," said Maggie.

"Promise?"

"I promise," said Maggie.

Mary Alice snuggled up in Brian's arms. And all three sat without talking until they heard thunder in the distance. "Sounds like rain is coming," said Brian. "Guess it's time for us to get cleaned up," as he began putting plates and cups in the trash can.

"Don't forget the ball" said Mary Alice, running to the grassy area to bring it back to Maggie.

As the three of them drove back home the rain began to fall. Mary Alice fell asleep in the backseat. Maggie and Brian were also exhausted, but Brian still had to drive Mary Alice to Missouri and face Jenny's parents tomorrow.

Chapter 10

Stan had never been so tired. His head ached as he poured the water in the coffee pot. He had only slept a couple of hours and now he had to drive to Pilot Ridge and face the Andersons. He wanted to give himself two hours so he could be careful. He didn't want to fall asleep at the wheel. He made eggs and toast. He knew it was important to eat and keep life as normal as possible. He left at 12:00 noon, but stopped at a market to buy gas, go to the men's room and get a Coke. Something about relieving himself cleared his head. He thought: *We can't let the news out about Jenny. We can't alert the person who killed her. He thinks he got away with it. We don't want him to run. There's a small cemetery on the Anderson property. We can bury her there in a private ceremony. I'll bring Jamie for the day. It'll be good for her to see her grandparents. Heaven only knows when she'll get to see them again.* Stan picked up the Coke cup as he pulled into the Anderson's yard. The sucking sounds of an empty cup echoed in his ears as yelping dogs, Martha and George met him on the porch.

"You're back so soon? Is there something wrong?" asked Martha.

"Yes," said Stan, folding his arms and looking at the road. "Here comes Sheriff Madden. There's something we have to tell you."

The sheriff came to the porch. "Come on in," said George. "I reckon we're about ready for anything you can lay on us."

"The test we did on Martha's hair and the corpse's hair matches," said Stan. "We're sure it's Jenny."

"I was afraid you were going to tell me that," said George. Martha was sitting in the chair by the fireplace, wringing her hands.

"She's my only baby. I don't know how I'll go on without her," said Martha.

"Because we're investigating her murder, we'll be unable to put her death on the news or have a big funeral. I don't want to alert the bastard who did this to her," said Stan.

"What'll we do for her?" asked Martha.

"What about that little cemetery on the back of the place. Are there any plots left?" asked Stan.

"Me and Martha plan to be buried there and there's room for two or three more. Do you want Jenny to be buried there?" asked George.

"That would be good," said Stan. You know she kept her Anderson name, so it'll be fitting for her to be buried in the Anderson family cemetery."

"You mean she didn't take your name?" said Martha. "You are married, aren't you?"

"Yes, it's the nature of my work. It's best if family connections are not made too public," said Stan.

"When will we do this?" asked George.

"Give me three days. The coroner will have her body delivered on Wednesday. George, do you think you can get some of the boys to dig the grave?" asked Stan. "Jamie wants to come. I'll have to go get her."

"Shouldn't be any problem getting the grave dug." said George.

"Be careful about who you ask to help. We still don't know who killed Jenny," said Stan.

"Bless her heart, Jenny's little girl'll be here. It's been so long since we've seen her.

"We'll spend Wednesday night. My job is demanding and Jamie will have to go back to Missouri. You know this is not over. I have to keep Jamie safe," said Stan.

"Is there anything else we can do?" asked George.

"No, just have the grave ready by Wednesday morning. The sooner we finish the burial the better. It needs to be over before the week-end and it's best if you and Martha don't talk about it," said Stan.

"Ain't nobody around here to tell," said George.

"You never know who you're talking to. Until we find out who did this to Jenny everyone is a suspect," said Stan.

"Ok, we won't talk about it, will we Martha?"

Martha didn't say anything, only nodded.

Stan barely arrived in Durant before the coroner's lab closed. He arranged for Jenny's body to be delivered to Pilot Ridge on Wednesday morning. It would be a closed casket. The coroner handed Stan the ring Jenny had been wearing.

"Thank you," said Stan. He thought, but did not say, *"My daughter will want this someday."*

When at home, Stan held the ring in his hand. Jenny would never wear his ring again. He would never see her cocky smile or feel her hand in his. *How can I move past my grief? How can I get past knowing you were murdered? How will I find your killer?* Stan folded the message from Washington D.C. and put it in the bedside table drawer. He would put the message in the safety deposit box at the bank, or maybe with J. Morris. There was so much to think about. His mind was cloudy. Maybe sleep would help. He laid down. He tried, but when he closed his eyes, Jenny was there.

I remember the first time I saw you. We were at a state department party. J. Morris and I were there together. We'd both finished college and he'd gone into law and I'd gone into law enforcement. He was working as a prosecutor for the state and was invited to their Christmas party. I was his plus-one. Neither of us was dating anyone at the time. You were standing by the punch bowl talking to a friend dressed in a red pantsuit. Your fingernails and toenails were painted green—appropriate for Christmas.

"I always wear green nail polish," you said. The way you cocked your head, swinging your long black hair around when you talked made my heart beat faster. I wanted to go to you. I wanted to know you. When I introduced myself, you didn't seem interested but I knew I had to get to know you better.

I asked your name. As I lay there in bed, I heard you say: "Virginia, but my friends call me Jenny." I wanted to call you Jenny. I wanted to be your friend, no I wanted more. I asked you to dance and you did.

Before the night was over, she had agreed to have lunch with me. She was cautious. I admired her toughness. She never bent to my wooing. She remained cool even when I kissed her. When I told her I was a CIA officer, she never flinched. She was willing to live in obscurity and that's what we built our marriage on. We married on the run and bought a little house under an assumed name because the case I was working on was dangerous. I didn't want to be traceable.

"I never let anyone at work know I was married. You gave me a beautiful ring unidentifiable as a wedding ring." she said.

"And now you'll never wear it again." Stan saw Jenney standing before him dressed in a beautiful red dress, but then she vanished.

It was an hour before Stan roused. There was so much to think about, so much to do. How was he ever going to get through this? How was he going to breathe? He still had to drive to Missouri.

Brian called Maggie. "I've made the arrangements. I'm going after Mary Alice tomorrow. I know she'll want you to come to the burial, but I think it's best if you're not identified with Jenny in any way."

"I understand," said Maggie. "Will I get to see Jamie? I mean Mary Alice?"

"When did you find out?" asked Brian.

"Jamie told me right after Christmas. I think she just had to tell somebody. I told her she still has to be Mary Alice until you tell her it's alright to be Jamie again," said Maggie.

"Thank you for keeping our secret. This will all be over someday, and we can go back to normal, whatever that it," said Brian.

"Do you think we can sneak in a visit or is it too dangerous?"

"What if you ride up to Missouri with me? I'm so tired, you can keep me awake driving back. You and Jamie'll have three hours to talk. You've been a life-saver for her. I don't know what I would have done without you," said Brian.

"I'll call in for a personal day off," said Maggie.

"I'll pick you up at five in the morning. Maybe we can be back here right after lunch. I have some things I want to check out at the office. Will it be alright if Jamie stays with you a few hours after we get back?" asked Brian.

"You know it will," said Maggie.

Chapter 11

Just as Maggie hung up, her phone rang again. "Hi Maggie, it's Junior. We made it home alright. It was really good to see Daddy and Mr. Sutton. Your daddy has a surprise for you," said Junior.

"Do you know what it is?" asked Maggie.

"Well, yeah I do, but I don't want to ruin his surprise," said Junior. "Are you still coming to Boonetown this week-end?"

"I still plan to come," said Maggie.

"Then, you can wait that long to find out. Anyway, Daddy and Mr. Sutton said they have something else they need to talk to both of us about. They said it's a secret they've shared for over thirty years. Do you know what it is?" asked Junior.

"I don't have a clue. Something they did when they were kids, I guess," said Maggie.

"I might know what it is. I was at Daddy Alb's wake when I was ten or eleven years old and they talked about secrets. They told me about one secret. They've probably forgotten they told me. For a kid, it was pretty intriguing. They found the Civil War treasure. It wasn't a lot of money, but back then it seemed like a lot. It helped Daddy buy his farm. We still have one of those silver dollars in the sugar bowl at home. Daddy said he would never spend it," said Junior.

"That's most likely it. They were good friends back then. I'm glad they've reconnected. I'll let you know if I can't come to Boonetown, but right now I think I'll be there," said Maggie.

"See you on Saturday," said Junior.

"See you," said Maggie.

Maggie spent another long night, tossing and turning. She couldn't sleep, so she got up early. She was ready and sitting on her porch waiting for Brian. The sky was just beginning to turn blue in the East, but it was still dark in Durant. Brian drove into the driveway, headlights illuminating the porch. Maggie jumped up from her chair where she was half asleep and ran to the car.

"Good morning! Looks like it'll be a sunny day," said Maggie.

"Good morning, thanks for going with me. I'm a grown man for God's sake, but this has brought me down," said Brian.

"I'm glad to help," said Maggie, as she climbed into the passenger side.

Brian turned the radio on a jazz station. "Do you enjoy jazz?" he asked.

"I love jazz," said Maggie. They listened, neither one wanting to interrupt the music.

"I've been thinking," said Brian. "I'll introduce you to Jamie's grandparents because they'll be receiving mail from you each week. It'll be good for them to put a face on what's happening. I guess they already got one package?"

"I sent one the end of last week. They should've gotten Jamie's schoolwork this past Monday," said Maggie. "Jamie is a good student and she'll do the work. I may have trouble keeping up with her."

"I have faith in you. I know you'll do the right thing for Jamie. She loves you so much. I don't know what we'll do when she goes to second grade. We may have to take you with us," said Brian with a curious smile.

"I feel the same way. I would have advanced Jamie before now, but I couldn't bear the thought of letting her go," said Maggie.

My parents will be happy to meet you. They say Jamie talks about you all the time," said Brian.

"I'll be happy to meet them, too. Now what are their names?"

"Hattie and James Turner," said Brian.

Turner? Not Scott? Thought Maggie. *Maybe his mother has been married twice and her first husband was named Scott?* Maggie decided to stop asking questions. Brian had already told her he would tell her what he could.

Jamie came running out the front door. "Daddy, I've been waiting for you all morning," looking past her daddy, "Ms. Maggie! You came, too. Thank you," throwing her arms around Maggie.

"Let's go in and see Papa and Grandma for a minute before we get back on the road," said Brian. He introduced them to Maggie, and they talked about Jamie's school work. "Jamie doesn't have any trouble finishing all her work," said Brian's mother.

"I'll try to send some work that'll challenge her," said Maggie.

"Not everybody would help like you're doing," said Brian's mother.

"Hey, girl, are you ready to go? Bring the dollhouse and you and Ms. Maggie can play with it on the way back," said Brian. Mother, I'm sorry you and Daddy can't come to the burial. We have to keep this low key."

"We understand," said Brian's daddy. "Just keep our little girl safe."

"I'm trying," said Brian. "You're helping. I appreciate all you're doing."

Maggie and Jamie crawled into the backseat together with the dollhouse, books and other toys. Jamie clutched Maggie's hand. "Shall we read a book? How about *Winnie The Pooh*?" asked Maggie. "Do you like honey?" poking Jamie on her nose.

"I like Winnie The Pooh. He's a Willy Neilly Silly Ole Bear," said Jamie, laughing. Brian smiled. Maggie and Jamie sang, *The Wheels on the Bus* and Brian sang along. He was not falling asleep.

"Jamie, is it alright with you if Daddy goes to work for a while? Ms. Maggie said you can stay at her house until I get back."

"Yes, yes, yes," said Jamie. "Can I spend the night, and can Ms. Maggie go with me to say good-bye to Mommy?"

"Sweetheart, I would love to go with you tomorrow, but the other boys and girls are expecting me back at school tomorrow. You know I have to go and teach my class," said Maggie.

"It'll be alright. I'll get to visit with Grandpa and Grandma Anderson. Grandma says Mommy was her little girl," said Jamie.

"Don't forget I'll send you a 'love note' every week when I send your lessons," said Maggie.

"Jamie, behave yourself. I'll be back in a couple of hours," said Brian.

"Ok, Daddy," said Jamie, as she reached for Maggie's hand.

"I love you," said Jamie.

"I love you more," said Maggie, as they went into the house. "How would you like to help me make dinner? We'll have it ready when your daddy comes and you can eat before you go home."

"Yeah, what will we cook?"

"What do you like, how about hamburgers and chocolate chip cookies?"

"Yeah, can I stir the cookies?"

"Absolutely," said Maggie. "And measure the milk and break the eggs. You can just make the cookies and I'll make the hamburgers. Can you read the recipe?"

"Yes, I can read it," she said, taking the recipe book out of Maggie's hand. "Where do you keep your flour?"

Maggie helped Jamie find all the ingredients for the cookies and began slicing tomatoes and onions for the hamburgers. She remembered she had some frozen French fries in the freezer. "Do you like fried potatoes?" asked Maggie.

"French fries are my favorite," said Jamie.

Brian arrived just as they finished cooking. Jamie was setting the table. "Does the fork go on the left?"

"You've got it," said Maggie.

Jamie finished her hamburger, went into the living room and began drawing with the paper and crayons Maggie had left on the coffee table.

"Food never tasted so good," said Brian "I was going to stop by the Dairy Queen."

"Is there anything new?" asked Maggie.

"I shouldn't be talking about this. You know you have to keep anything I say under wraps. Sometimes I forget. You seem to bring the 'tell all' out in me," he said, smiling.

"I hope whatever you find proves to be helpful," said Maggie. "And, you know anything you tell me will remain confidential."

"I hate to eat and run, but we need to prepare for tomorrow and get a good night's rest," said Brian. "I hope you're not offended."

"Of course, I understand completely," said Maggie, as Brian and Jamie left.

Maggie cleaned up the dishes and settled down to watch TV. A massage parlor had been raided in Durant on suspicion of prostitution. *I can't believe that would happen around here, she thought.* She turned the TV off and her thoughts quickly went back to Brian. She felt his pain. She wished she could help him, but how?

The Farm

Stan went to his office, closed the door and sat down at his desk. He put his head in his hands, closed his eyes and groaned. He sat there in the silence for twenty minutes before he heard a light peck on the door. "Come in," he said.

"Hey, man. What you doing in here with the lights off?" said Jeff Newman.

"I don't know, Jeff. I'm a mess."

Jeff turned the light on and pulled a chair up beside Stan. "I'm your boss, I'm not a counselor, but I am your friend, do you want to talk about it?"

"My wife is dead. We're laying her body to rest tomorrow. My daughter is six years old. I have to be strong for her, but worst of all I've met a woman I'm attracted to. Do you know how guilty I feel? My wife is not even in her grave and I have feelings for another woman? I don't know how to handle everything coming at me. What am I supposed to do?" said Stan.

"I've known you for a long time. You're not the kind of person who would cheat on his wife. Give it some time. Feelings are fresh. You've needed someone. This woman has obviously been there for you," said Jeff.

"She's Jamie's teacher," said Stan.

"There you go. She has helped you with Jamie. You shouldn't feel guilty. You're grateful for her help. That's likely all it amounts to. Give it some time. Put one foot in front of the other—one step at a time," said Jeff.

"Jamie's with her now. I told them I'd be gone a couple of hours. I have to get myself up and get going. Did you want something?" asked Stan.

"I have something I want to talk to you about, but it can wait. You have enough on your plate," said Jeff.

Jeff left Stan at his desk. Stan looked at the clock. He needed to hurry. Jamie would be worried. Just as he got up to leave the phone rang.

"This is Sheriff Madden. That latex glove we found near Jenny's body has a fingerprint on the inside."

"Do you have a match," asked Stan.

"No, we're working on it. I'll let you know," said Sheriff Madden.

"Thank you. Keep in touch" said Stan, as he hung up the phone and hurried out the door to pick up Jamie at Maggie's house.

Chapter 12

When Stan and Jamie arrived at the Anderson's house in Pilot Ridge there were three cars in the yard. "Get your sweater out of the car and put it on," said Stan. "It's cooler in the mountains. We'll be outside most of the day."

Jamie pulled her soft, pink sweater out of her bag. She looked pretty in pink with her dark hair glistening in the sun. "Do we leave the bag in the car?" asked Jamie.

"Yes, for now. We'll get it later after all these people leave," said Stan.

George came to the door. "We've got everything ready. Her body arrived about an hour ago. They took it to the graveside. What time do you want to start?"

"Whenever you're ready," said Stan. "Why are so many people here?"

"Martha said it wouldn't be right unless a Minister said a blessing over Jenny, so she invited the Methodist preacher to say a few words," said George.

"I thought it would be just family," said Brian, but forced himself to silence. What was done was done.

The neighborhood women were in the kitchen preparing food. They had set up a table made from sawhorses and boards outside to serve as the eating area. George had brought chairs from the church.

The circuit Methodist Minister was at the graveside. He had known Jenny from childhood. He baptized her when she was twelve.

"Thanks for officiating," said Stan.

"It's the downside of my job," said the pastor.

The women hurried to the graveside. There were eleven people in all. Brian knew it was too many, but there was nothing he could do about it now.

"I want to thank everyone for coming out to say good-bye to our little Jenny, today," said the pastor. "You're good people and Jenny was a good person. From the time she was twelve when I baptized her, she was always insightful and helpful. Now God has taken her to be with Him. Jesus said in the Gospel of John, chapter 14: *Let not your heart be troubled: ye believe in God, believe also in me. In my Father's house are many mansions: If it were not so, I would have told you. I go to prepare a place for you. And if I go and prepare a place for you, I will come again, and receive you unto myself; that where I am, there ye may be also.* Jenny is with the Lord, today. Walking on streets paved with gold. She has a mansion not made with hands. She will never be sad again. She will be filled with eternal happiness. We can't bring her back to us, but we will all experience death and go there to be with her and our blessed Lord. Thank you, Jesus, for preparing a place for us all. Amen.

Two of the ladies sang in beautiful harmony: *I've got a mansion, just over the hilltop in that bright land where we'll never grow old. And, someday yonder, we'll nevermore wonder, but walk on streets that are pure as gold.*

The ceremony took less than twenty minutes and then it was time to cover the casket. Each person walked by and threw in a handful of dirt. Jamie followed her daddy's example and threw in dirt and a flower she had picked in the yard. The neighbor men finished the job, packing the dirt down around the cedar casket, and shoveling the remainder of the dirt until the ground was level. George had carved a stone: Virginia Anderson, 1926-1959.

As Jamie and Stan were walking back to the house Jamie began to question: "Daddy, are the streets in Heaven really made out of gold?"

"I believe the Bible says that," said Stan. "But it could be just an example, like saying best place, ever."

"Is Mommy in the best place, ever?"

"Yes, I do believe Mommy is in the very best place," said Stan.

The women brought all the food to the outside table. A red checkered, feed sack, tablecloth covered the table. There was a mountain of fried chicken, macaroni and cheese, mashed potatoes, green beans, corn, and cornbread, along with cucumber and beet pickles Martha had made a huge chocolate cake and some of the women made pecan pies. It was a feast and a celebration party fit for Jenny. Jamie wondered where the ice cream was and Martha said, "I almost forgot. We made two freezers of ice cream this morning and they are wrapped in towels on the back porch. Yelling at George, "get the boys and bring out the ice cream, Jamie's ready for hers." George and Stan brought the ice cream freezers to the side yard. One was vanilla and the other strawberry. Jamie took vanilla.

After the neighbors left, George and Stan settled down in the rocking chairs on one end of the porch. Stan watched while Martha and Jamie snuggled in the porch swing. "I used to sit here with your mother and swing for hours," said Martha, arranging Jamie's hair and replacing the barrette.

"I love my dollhouse," said Jamie. "My little people love it, too. It'll be their home forever, but now the mommy can't play. I'll have to leave her in the spare room."

"She may be separated from her family, but she still loves them very much and they'll never forget her," said Martha.

"Her family loves her, too," said Jamie.

The swinging motion was making Jamie sleepy. She snuggled closer to Martha and drifted off. Martha was exhausted, too. She rested her head on Jamie's head. Memories of Jenny flashed through her mind. Her little girl was gone, but she had left a wonderful granddaughter to love. She softly praised God and thanked Him for His mercy.

After retiring early and arising early, both Stan and Jamie were ready to head back to Durant where they stopped to pick up a few more clothes for Jamie and immediately headed to Missouri. By now Jamie had come to expect she would be living with her grandparents in Missouri for a long time.

Chapter 13

Maggie told Junior she would meet him in Boonetown at the Drugstore around noon. When she arrived, Junior was sitting in the ole red truck in front of the Drugstore.

"What're you doing here in Daddy's truck? Where's Daddy?" asked Maggie.

"Your daddy hasn't arrived yet and my daddy went over to the garage for some grease for his wagon wheels," said Junior.

Just about that time Avery came driving up in his shiny new silver truck. The mischievous smile on his face told her everything. "Who are you?" laughed Maggie.

"Surprise," said Avery.

"This truck is gorgeous," said Maggie. "What does mother think about you getting a new truck?"

"Aw, she's ok," said Avery. "Come on and get in. I'll take you for a spin around town until Joe gets finished." Maggie hopped in and began fiddling with the knobs. "There's lots of things to play with."

"Hey, that's the heat, it's 80 degrees today. We won't need that," said Avery.

"What made you decide to buy a new truck?" asked Maggie.

"I figured a new truck every twenty years is about right," said Avery.

"What's Junior doing in the old truck?" asked Maggie.

"I decided we didn't need it anymore and I just up and gave it to him and Joe," said Avery. "I couldn't get nothing for it on the trade-in. I told Joe you'd probably pitch a fit. We've made a ton of memories in that old truck."

"You're right. I am sentimental about the truck, but I understand. Junior and Joe need transportation," said Maggie.

Joe was now waiting with Junior. Avery and Maggie drove up and parked beside them.

Maggie jumped out of the truck. "Let's go in the drugstore, sit at a table and have a Coke" she said.

"Wait," said Avery. "I'm not sure Junior and Joe will be served."

"This is Boonetown, of course they'll be served," said Maggie.

"No, Maggie. It's true we've never been able to sit down and drink a Coke in the drugstore.

"Well, that's just not right," said Maggie. "Come on. We won't stand for that kind of nonsense."

Avery and Joe reluctantly followed Junior and Maggie into the drugstore. Maggie marched over to a table in the front and said: "Will this one do?" The men came over and pulled out a chair, just as Jim from the slaughterhouse came into the store.

"Hey Maggie, what you doing here with niggers? I didn't know you're a nigger lover," said Jim.

"I didn't know you're a blooming idiot," said Maggie.

"I'm not eating in a place that serves niggers," said Jim.

"Suit yourself," said Maggie, pointing to Avery, Junior and Joe. "Sit down and I'll go to the counter and bring our Cokes back."

The young girl at the counter whispered to Maggie. "As long as no one else comes in, I won't say anything, but I would appreciate it if you would drink your Cokes and leave as quickly as possible." Maggie took the Cokes back to the table without replying. Anger boiled within her. She couldn't believe she had been so sheltered. She had not realized the extent of the black people's struggles.

"Some of the men at The Farm were talking about this very thing. Demonstrations are going to happen all over the country where black people go to a restaurant and demand to be served. They're going to change the way things are done and I believe today we've just started the movement," said Junior.

"Let's not push our luck," said Maggie. Looking at Joe and Avery, "what's this big secret you're wanting to share with us? Junior thinks he knows. He said you told him about the Civil War treasure. We think you probably forgot you told him."

"It's not that," said Avery, taking a big swig of his Coke. But you still need to keep that secret. The electric company could lay claim to the money. We found it on their property."

"We'd hate to have to help you pay that money back," said Maggie.

"What we have to tell you is a good bit more serious than that," said Joe.

"Well, for God's sake, tell us. I'm about to bust with curiosity," said Maggie.

Avery looked at Joe. "It has to do with who my Daddy is," said Joe.

"I heard a story about a man from across the tracks," said Maggie.

"Well, yes I heard that story, too and I believed it until I was married and Junior was already born, but that story wasn't true," said Joe.

"My daddy knew the truth," said Avery. Joe's mother, Sadie, told Daddy Alb and he left a letter telling us who Joe's daddy really is."

"You mean Daddy Alb is Joe's daddy and you are brothers?" said Maggie.

"No, let me finish," said Avery. Daddy Alb said his brother, Joseph, is Joe's daddy. His mother, Sadie, named her son Nuley Mac Joseph—Nuley after her deceased husband and Mac after my daddy, Albert Mac Sutton, but in fact, because their last name is Joseph and Mac means 'son of' Sadie had named her son 'Son of Joseph'." The truth was right there all along."

"Maggie looked at Junior and counted on her fingers. That makes us third cousins. Our daddies are first cousins. Can you believe that?"

"The way my life has been going lately, I can believe just about anything," said Junior, finishing his Coke. Maggie and the men left the drugstore just as some others were coming in. Maggie and Junior walked out hand in hand. People craned their necks looking. One woman ran headfirst into the door.

"Maybe we should keep their secret," said Maggie. "You don't want to do anything that might get you fired from your new job before you've had a chance to prove yourself."

"You're right," said Junior. "We'll keep this one under wraps."

As Avery got in his new truck to leave, he reached over and rolled the window down. "Hey Junior, the boys are coming up tonight to go coon hunting. Bring ole Blue and go with us."

"I might just do that," said Junior, as they both pulled away and headed home.

The Farm

Stan had a restless night, so he went to his office early. There was something on his mind, something he was leaving undone. What was it? Sitting at his desk, drinking his morning coffee, it dawned on him. He needed to talk to his lawyer. J. Morris would be at work soon.

Jenny and Stan had always maintained separate social contacts, separate business contacts and separate identities. No one at the State Department knew much about Jenny's personal life. She had been keeping books for the governor for the past twelve years. Jenny was an independent woman who prided herself on self-sufficiency. When she went missing, Stan had called and spoken to the Human Resources Department asking for an extended leave of absence. She had more than enough vacation days to take care of her absence. Although Stan and Jenny kept separate relationships, they did have the same lawyer. J. Morris Higgins, Esq. had drawn up their wills and Power of Attorney documents. He had been a witness at their marriage.

"Is J. Morris in?" asked Stan.

"Yes sir. He's with a client, said the receptionist.

"This is Stan. When he's finished have him call me. He knows my number."

"I'll let him know you called," said the receptionist.

Stan picked up the *Psychology Magazine-A Guide to Happy Living* that he found in the visitor lounge. What makes people do what they do? He wondered. He knew he was driven by the desire to bring wrong doers to justice and he also knew sometimes his viewpoint was clouded by his narrow perspective. He read a short article on how to find release from inferiority feelings and another on how women think differently than men. Guess that's why men say they can never understand women, almost laughing.

The phone rang. "How are you?" asked J. Morris.

"I've been better. It's alright if you charge me for this call. It's business. I'm sorry I didn't make an appointment," said Stan.

"I just happen to have a couple of hours before I'm due in court," said J. Morris. "Let's go to lunch and talk."

"I would prefer to see you in private," said Stan. "Can you come by my office?"

"This sounds serious. I'll be there in about fifteen minutes."

Later, the men sat down across from each other. Stan lowered his head and stared at the floor.

"Old friend, you're beginning to scare me. What's going on?" asked J. Morris.

"Have you heard? Jenny's dead." said Stan.

"I knew she was missing. I'm so sorry, what. . ."

"She was murdered."

"How, When? Who? I'm sorry. I'm stunned. I'm working on three other cases right now and just haven't had time to check on Jenny."

"She was strangled just before Christmas. We only found her body a couple of weeks ago. The bastard threw her body in Salt Creek up in the mountains. The thing we don't know is who. We've kept it a secret. Sheriff Madden is still investigating.

"You won't have to do it. It'll be the state's case," said J. Morris.

"I want to know we have enough evidence to convict before we make an arrest. I don't want the guy to get off on some technicality," said Stan.

"You're a wise man. You're doing the right thing. You know I met with Jenny a couple of months before Christmas. She had a sealed envelope she wanted me to keep for her. She said something to the effect if she was fired, she wanted documented evidence to share when she brought suit against the state," said J. Morris. "I brought your file and Jenny's file with me."

He opened Jenny's file and handed Stan the envelope.

"I'll read this in private. It's the last word I'll have from Jenny. I don't feel much like eating. Maybe we can go to lunch another day."

"I understand. Stay in touch. We'll need to go over Jenny's will."

"When they make an arrest, I'll call you. You can help me build my case. It won't be easy," said J. Morris.

"The one I suspect is well known. He has influence in high places. The case needs to be solid," said Stan.

"We'll make it stick. Just let me know," said J. Morris. "When you're ready, we'll go over Jenny's will, as they shook hands and J. Morris left for court.

Stan sat starring at the letter. There was nothing to do but open the envelope.

Stan took a letter opener and split the envelope open, pulled out a single sheet of paper and read: *I'm leaving this information with my lawyer, J. Morris Higgins on November 10th 1959. I'm having trouble with a man at work. He's been making advances and flirting with me for some time now. These are the events and dates I remember:*

October 22, we were in a meeting together and he winked at me.

October 27, he sat down by me and talked, touching my arm in a familiar way.

October 30, he walked by and popped me on my bottom and laughed.

November 1st, he pressed himself against me in a crowded elevator and I could feel his hard penis against my backside.

November 5th, I was required to go with him to another office for a meeting. I found out later he had requested I go with him. He stopped the car in the park and unzipped his pants to show himself. I told him in no uncertain terms I was not interested. He slapped me. I jumped out of the car and walked, no ran, back to the office.

This man is high-up in the Legislature and old enough to be my daddy. If I complain to human resources I won't be heard. It'll be his word against mine and who is going to believe a bookkeeper over a state congressman. I feel I'll have to take matters into my own hands. I'm not sure what I'll do yet short of bodily harm, but if he approaches me again, I'm going to do something. He's a dangerous man and I will not let him get away with this. His name is John Butcher.

Stan laid the paper on his desk. He had no idea Jenny was going through such a trial. He had been too busy with his own work to notice and of course she wouldn't bother him with her troubles. Rage rose in his gut. He should just find the bastard and string him up by his balls and tell him if he ever touches another woman, he'll kill him. Jenny was a sweet, forward, friendly woman. Maybe he misread her, but no, he went overboard even if he thought Jenny encouraged him. But there was no reason to think Jenny gave him any encouragement. Jenny was right. Her voice would not have been heard. What could he do about it? Jenny was gone. There would be no justice for her. This man would be left to prey on other young women.

Stan sat at his desk thinking, trying to make since of this information. He needed another opinion. He needed to talk to Maggie.

Chapter 14

Maggie hurried to the bathroom to change clothes, freshen her makeup and comb her hair before putting a drop of Blue Waltz perfume on her wrist. Brian had called and was coming over. She wondered why she was so excited. There was no way a man like Brian would be attracted to a girl like her, so ordinary, so plain.

The doorbell rang. Brian entered the room. "God, something smells good," said Brian.

"Just a little something from a bottle," laughed Maggie. "Come in and have a seat. What's going on?"

"My lawyer came by my office today and he had a note Jenny left with him before she died. It's enlightening and enraging. I just wanted a woman to read the note and help me discern how to react. Brian handed the note to Maggie and she began to read:

"Jenny is absolutely right," said Maggie. "Women don't have much clout in the workplace. She has dated each incident and explained what happened. She left the information in a safe place so it wouldn't be discovered at work. I agree with her this man's actions are progressive. He's getting braver by the week. And she provided you with a name. Have you heard of him? John Butcher, wait! That name sounds familiar. I need to speak with Daddy before I say anymore," said Maggie.

"Then, she did the right thing? I only wish she could've come to me," said Brian.

"She was a very brave woman," said Maggie.

"Maybe too brave," said Brian. "I'll be glad when Junior is finished with school. He can help me with Jenny's case and a lot of others. He's moving in with me tomorrow. School begins on Monday."

"You and Junior should come over for dinner tomorrow night. We'll celebrate his new position," said Maggie.

"Can we have roast beef?" asked Brian, with a twinkle in his eye.

"Roast beef it is. At least you'll have one good meal this week," said Maggie. "I've been meaning to talk to you about Jamie. We're having an IQ test and she'll need to be tested. When will you go to Missouri again?"

"I was planning on going this Saturday," said Brian.

"Can I go with you? The test will take about two hours. I could let your mother administer the test, but it would be illegal. It's best if I give the test. I already know I want her to skip second grade. Her test scores will be the rationale for advancing her to third grade," said Maggie.

"Is it alright with you if I hang around and watch TV with you? This whole thing with Jenny has really freaked me out," said Brian.

"I'll make us some popcorn," said Maggie.

"That sounds good. I don't think I've eaten anything all day," said Brian. "I can handle serious cases, but when it's personal it hits you in the gut."

"I can only imagine," said Maggie, as they settled in to watch a movie, eating popcorn and drinking beer. The movie was a comedy. Brian even found himself laughing. But, before the movie was over, he was stretched out on the couch sound asleep. Maggie brought a blanket and covered him up before she put her pajamas on and went to bed.

At 5:00 a.m. Maggie got up to go to the bathroom when she noticed Brian was still there. She watched as he pried his eyes open and looked around. He got to his feet and headed toward the door.

"Wait right there, mister," said Maggie, standing in her bedroom door in her pajamas. "You can't hog my couch, eat my popcorn and run off without saying good-bye."

"Maggie, I'm so sorry and embarrassed," said Brian.

"You're exhausted. You really need to let this thing with Jenny rest a while. Go help Junior move in and I'll see you at 6:00 for dinner. Don't think about the case today and we'll go to Missouri tomorrow. It'll be wonderful to see Jamie and relax away from the stress," said Maggie.

"You're right.," said Brian, walking over to Maggie and giving her a little hug. "You're a lifesaver."

Maggie retrieved the roast from the freezer. After it thawed a bit, she put it in the crockpot. It was much easier not to have to attend to it all day. She sat down with her bowl of cereal and turned on the television—cartoons, children's programs. She wondered what Jamie liked to watch on Saturday. *Would she go for the princess films or the knockdown, drag'em in flicks?* The thought of spending time with Jamie made her happy. Her cereal bowl was empty. It was going on nine o'clock, time to get dressed and get busy. But there was something she needed to do. Oh yes, she wanted to talk to her daddy about the name that seemed so familiar.

"Hi Daddy, how are you this morning?" asked Maggie.

"I'm alright, just a little tired. How are you?" asked Avery.

"Doing fine, do you remember telling me about the 'big shots' from Durant who have been hunting with you and Mr. Anderson lately? What's their names? I can't remember what you told me. Somebody I know may know one of them," said Maggie.

"The main one is John Butcher. He's a state congressman, I think. Right now, I can't remember his friend's name either. He's in the music business. I think he's a song-writer," said Avery.

"I'm writing that down. My memory is bad nowadays," said Maggie. Is Mama alright? Everything else going ok?"

"Your mama is fine as she can be. I'm just trying to get Banjo ready for the coonhound trials next week. John Butcher says he has a good chance of winning. That would really be something. A little fellow like me having a champion coonhound!" said Avery.

"If Banjo wins it won't have anything to do with what John Butcher thinks. It'll be because you've put in the work it takes to train a dog properly. You and Banjo deserve to win and I'm rooting for you," said Maggie. "Junior starts training for his new job on Monday. I'm having him over tonight for dinner to celebrate."

"Now I don't want to tell you what to do, but people don't know about your kinship. The neighbors might think you're dating a black man. Be careful. I don't know how some people'll react," said Avery.

"Let them react. It's none of their business," said Maggie.

"Just be careful," said Avery.

"Always," said Maggie. "I love you. Tell Mama I love her. See you soon."

That is his name, thought Maggie. *This is more serious than I had thought. Daddy's mixed up with an awful man and he doesn't have a clue.*

Maggie put potatoes, carrots and onions in the roast and opened a can of green beans. The men would probably want bread. Around two in the afternoon she made a quick run to the store to get rolls and lemons for sweet tea. Ice cream would make a good dessert. She always had ice cream. Some days she needed comfort and ice cream was her 'go to' comfort food. She was beginning to set the table when the doorbell rang. Looking at her watch, it was 6:00 p.m. Where had the time gone?

"Hey guys, come on in. Dinner's almost ready. The time slipped up on me," said Maggie.

"Hey, it smells good," said Junior. "Don't think I've eaten since breakfast."

"I had a sandwich around noon, so I'm hungry," said Brian. "Thanks for having us over."

"Glad to oblige," said Maggie. "I don't mind cooking. Hope it's worth eating."

"So far everything I've eaten you've cooked has been delicious," said Brian. "I'm not much of a cook. Every now and again I try to make something, usually when I'm desperate—sick of hamburgers and fries."

"I can cook eggs," said Junior.

"That's good to know. Maybe you can make breakfast for us some morning," said Brian.

"Set the table," said Maggie, handing Brian a stack of plates and silverware,

"Can do," laughed Brian, taking the plates and placing them on the table.

"What can I do?" asked Junior.

"Help me put this roast on the platter while I get the green beans. Oops! The rolls are about to burn.

Take them out of the oven. Hurry!" said Maggie. "Getting everything to come out at the same time is my problem."

"Boy, those rolls smell good," said Junior.

"It's the alcohol in the yeast," said Maggie. "Looks like we're ready to eat."

Maggie could tell she would have no problem with leftovers. She had forgotten just how much guys could eat.

"God, this is good," said Brian.

"I'm enjoying every bite," said Junior.

"Well, don't get used to it. It'll be your turn next when you start making money."

"I'll do my best," said Junior, smiling.

Maggie made sure the men helped with the dishes before they retired to the den.

Looking at Junior, "Are you excited about tomorrow?" Brian asked.

"Well, yes and I guess a little anxious," said Junior. "I don't know exactly what to expect."

"It'll all be new at first. You've had more experience than most of the young guys. The only thing is you will be the only black man attending the class. There is one other black man in the CIA. You're not the first. The white guys may be a little prejudiced. Oh, damn. Why am I sugar coating this? You may experience down right prejudice. They may call you names, even try to discourage you from being an agent. It won't be easy," said Brian.

"I ought to take Maggie with me. She tore into a man in the drugstore when he called me a nigger and said he wouldn't eat in a place where I was eating," said Junior.

"I've never heard such nonsense. That idiot had no right to be talking like that. He's just stupid," said Maggie, entering the room.

"Don't be too hard on him," said Junior. "He was high."

"How do you know he was high?" asked Maggie.

"Didn't you see the tracks on his arms? He's a heroin addict," said Junior.

"That's exactly the attitude and the expertise that'll get you through narcotic school," said Brian. "Where do you think he gets his drugs?"

"I have my suspicion. I probably know," said Junior.

"You care to tell me?" said Brian.

"I'm working on an angle. I'll let you know when I get it figured out," said Junior.

Maggie interrupted, "I almost forgot to tell you. I called Daddy. The man that hunts with him from Durant is John Butcher."

"I met him," said Junior. "Him and that songwriter guy must be lovers. I followed them to the truck one night when we were coon hunting and I saw them hugging. I didn't stay long. I didn't want them to know I saw them."

"John Butcher is becoming more interesting by the minute. Junior, do you think you can go coon hunting a little more often so you can keep an eye on him?" said Brian.

"Actually, my dog is registered for the coonhound trials in Durant next Saturday. Mr. Sutton trained Blue and thought he ought to participate. I don't know much about coon hunting, but I reckon Blue knows," said Junior, laughing. "But I don't know about this hunting thing. That night I went with the fellows, we heard a big cat in the Jungle. His cry was 'hair-raising'. At least Mr. Sutton had the wisdom to get us out of there fast."

"Maggie and I have to leave at 5:00 a.m. to go to Missouri. We had better call it a night," said Brian.

"Sorry to eat and run," said Junior. "Thanks for doing this for me. You're right, it'll be my turn next."

"Don't forget your cap," said Brian, as he and Junior opened the door to leave. The moon was up and shining bright like a street lamp. Brian's heart felt light, even cozy. He looked back and saw Maggie walking back to the kitchen. Her black hair glistened. Her skirt dropped loosely around her hips. He wanted to stay. He closed the door and ambled to the car.

Chapter 15

Five o'clock came way too early. Maggie jumped out of bed at 4:30 and hurried to get in the shower. After changing clothes three times she dressed in black slacks and a red long-sleeved pull-over. Her hair was still damp when she poured her cereal. There was barely enough milk. She would need to remember to go to the store before Monday morning. She had only taken a couple of bites when she heard Brian blow his car horn. *He's early,* she thought. *I'm not even ready.* She looked out the window. The neighbor across the street turned on his porch light. *We're waking the whole neighborhood. Wonder what my nosey neighbor is thinking? I need to get a move on. Now where did I put that test? If I forget the test this whole trip is a bust.* Maggie grabbed the test, her purse and her make-up case. Hands full, she stumbled out the door.

"Sorry, I'm running a bit late," said Maggie.

"I may be a tiny bit early," said Brian. "I see your neighbor is keeping an eye on you."

Maggie climbed in the car, fastened her seatbelt and lowered the passenger mirror to begin putting on her make-up. "He should mind his own business, said Maggie. "I must look a sight."

"You look just fine to me," said Brian, smiling, as he pulled onto Route 60. The country road was woven through forest and over bubbling streams and into Illinois before they reached Missouri. Although Kentucky bordered Missouri there was no direct road from Kentucky to Missouri. The morning was misty, eerie, and lovely. Not many cars on the road at five in the morning. Brian turned the headlights on and slowed the car. Although he had driven this section of the route many times, the curves came up fast and his Lincoln didn't corner as well as he would like. There was only one ferryboat that took people across the Mississippi River from 9:00 a.m. until 5:00 p.m. which meant driving fifty miles out of the way and another hour of travel time.

"Oh, look. There's a bear," said Brian. Maggie came alive and looked, but she was too late. The bear lumbered across the road and into the underbrush. "The mountains are beautiful this time of day with the fog and all."

"It's still dark, guess I haven't gotten my eyes open yet," said Maggie.

"If you need to, just go to sleep. I'll be ok," said Brian.

"If I go to sleep, will you go to sleep?" asked Maggie, teasing.

"I'm not sleepy," said Brian.

Maggie pulled her feet up under her legs and laid her seat back. "This big ole car does have its advantages," she said, as she drifted off. Light filtered through the darkness as the sun edged over the mountain behind them.

The sun-beams in the window awakened her. "How long was I out?" she asked.

"About an hour. Did you know you snore?" said Brian.

"I do not," said Maggie, sitting up and smoothing her hair.

"I brought us a Granola Bar if you want one. They're in that bag right behind the seat,"said Brian.

"Don't mind if I do," said Maggie, reaching for the bag.

"There's a little bait shop just around the corner. I'll stop and get us a cup of coffee," said Brian.

"You really do know this road," said Maggie. "Yes, I would like a cup of coffee and a bathroom if they have one."

"They do," said Brian, as he pulled in to stop.

When Maggie came out of the bathroom, Brian was at the counter buying coffee. "What do you want in your coffee?" asked Brian.

"Nothing, just black," said Maggie.

"Two black coffees," said Brian, to the young man behind the counter.

They were soon in the car and on their way. The trees hung over the road in places and the curves seemed to bend backward to meet. The countryside was cool and green.

"Hand me one of those bars," said Brian. "I eat these on the run all the time."

"You really do live a busy, mysterious life," said Maggie. "What exactly do you do?"

"I work at The Farm and sometimes go out of town on business," said Brian. "I was too busy when Jenny was alive to pay attention to what was happening to her. That hurts. I wish I had done more to protect her."

"I know what you're going through. When Tom died, I was at a loss too," said Maggie.

"Tom? Who's Tom?"

"Tom was my husband. He was killed in Vietnam. We buried him the week before you brought Jamie to my class."

"I can't believe it. There I go again. I've been so wrapped up in my own problems I haven't even noticed your feelings." But Brian's feelings were not just about neglecting Maggie's feelings. The name, Tom Adams, triggered a deeper anxiety—pain even.

"Jamie and you have brought new energy into my life," said Maggie. "I have learned to love your little girl. There's something about her I can't explain. She just touches my heart."

"I don't know what Jamie would have done without you. And I'll admit it, you have helped me, too. I don't know how I would have survived all this time without your support," said Brian. "What was Tom like?"

"He was handsome, strong and quiet. He always said, better to be thought a fool than open your mouth and prove it," said Maggie. "He was a Second Lieutenant in the Army. He received an ROTC commission. We only dated a few months before we married and he was sent to Vietnam in about three months after we married. We bought our house and some furniture and were beginning to settle in when he had to leave."

"You must miss him," said Brian.

"He was married to the Army. You know when they say jump, you say how high? I really didn't know him all that well. After he arrived in Vietnam, we wrote letters, but you can't say much in a letter. Besides that, I think all outgoing and incoming letters are read by inspectors," said Maggie.

"I know about keeping secrets," said Brian. "And I also know about superiors inspecting your correspondence."

"Are they listening now?"

"Probably," said Brian.

"Hello, whoever you are. I'm not going to tell you anything important," said Maggie, laughing.

"We're almost there. Thank you for doing this for Jamie. She'll be so proud to spend time with you. How long did you say it will take?" asked Brian.

"The test will take about two hours," said Maggie.

"Mom said she'll fix lunch and right after we eat we can head back if that's alright with you."

"That'll get us home before dark. I'll have some work to do to prepare for class tomorrow," said Maggie. "And, I have to run by the store. What's on your agenda?"

"Not much to do on Sunday. Junior will be home. Guess we'll go over some pointers for his school. I'm so proud of him and the courage he shows. It's not an easy time for black people. There's a lot of unrest," said Brian. Junior will face prejudice, but he seems to understand and knows what he'll have to do to make it. He'll be a good officer.

"I know he'll do well," said Maggie, as Brian pulled the car into his parent's driveway.

Jamie and her grandpa were waiting on the front porch. As soon as the car stopped Jamie ran to hug Brian and Maggie. "I'm glad you're here," she said.

Mrs. Turner came to the door. "You're here. Thank God. I heard on the radio there was a wreck on Route 60 and I was just praying it wasn't you."

"We're fine," said Brian, giving his mother a hug. It must have happened back of us. We didn't see evidence of a wreck anywhere on the way. It's foggy, lucky to have low-beam headlights on my car. Dad, how've you been?"

"Fair to middling," said his daddy. Brian had informed his parents and Jamie to call him Brian around Maggie.

"Do you want something to eat before you start the test," asked Brian's mother, "I've got chocolate chip cookies right out of the oven."

"That sounds divine," said Maggie.

Jamie brought a saucer with six cookies on it. "Is it ok if I eat some while taking the test?" she asked.

"I don't see why not," said Maggie.

"What do you want to drink?" asked Brian's mother.

"Black coffee or a coke or just water, whatever you have is fine," said Maggie. "Jamie, what are you drinking?"

"Guess I'll take milk," said Jamie.

Maggie and Jamie took their cookies and milk to Jamie's room. Let's go to the 'little girl's room' before we start," said Maggie. "We'll take a half-time break, but other than that we'll not be allowed to talk. You must read the instructions carefully and complete the test without my help. Do you understand?"

"Yes, ma'am," said Jamie.

"It's 9:00 o'clock. At 10:00 we'll take a fifteen-minute break. Here's your test and number two pencil. You read the questions and fill in the circle that is beside the right answer," said Maggie, opening the test to the first page, pointing out the circles beside the answers.

"I understand," said Jamie.

Maggie opened the blinds to give more light. "Ready?"

"Ready," said Jamie, smiling.

"Go," said Maggie.

Jamie picked up her pencil and began reading the questions and filling in the circles. Maggie sat down by the window and began leafing through the *Good Housekeeping Magazine* she picked up from the coffee table in the living room.

It was two o'clock before dinner was eaten and Maggie and Brian were ready to head back to Durant.

"I don't want you to go," said Jamie, holding on to Brian.

"You know I'd love to stay with you, but Maggie and I have to get back to work," said Brian.

"Look for my next package. I'll send a special surprise," said Maggie. "You know next week is the last week of school for this year. I'm counting on you being back in Durant when school starts back in the fall."

"I can't wait to see the surprise," said Jamie.

"Heads up, it'll be here soon. I love you," said Maggie.

"Love you, too. Bye Daddy. I love you," said Jamie.

"You're my baby. I love you. We'll be together soon," said Brian, as he and Maggie hurried to the car.

It was Sunday afternoon. It looked like everybody was out for a drive, tractors, slow moving trucks and junk-rattle-trap cars all moving at a snail pace.

"There's a law. If you have 10 cars behind you, you're supposed to pull over and let people pass," said Brian, frustrated. Soon there was a scenic overlook with a hiking trail that ran alongside the road. Brian pulled the car over and opened the door. "I've got to take a breather."

Maggie got out of the car with him. "Let's take a walk down the trail and maybe by the time we're back the traffic will be gone."

About ten yards into the woods sat an inviting park bench. Maggie walked over and sat down motioning Brian to join her. "Do you run?" he asked.

"I try to run every day, but some days, like today I miss," said Maggie. "Do you run?"

"Yes, most days and I exercise at the gym. See my muscles," rolling up his sleeve to show off his biceps. Maggie reached over and pinched his arm. "That's some hard muscle. You must have worked on that one for a long time," said Maggie. "Did Jenny like that you were pumped up?"

"You know, I don't know. We never talked about it. I think she worked out, too, but I don't know where. We were both too involved in our work. When I was home, we only had dinner together three or four times a week. If I was late, I knew she would have something left for me and if she was late, I often ran out for a bite and brought her back a sandwich.

"How did Jamie change your lives? Surely Jenny had to let the people at work know she was married when she was pregnant?" said Maggie.

"We kept our marriage a secret so we would not be identified as a couple, so at about six months, before she was showing big, Jenny applied for sick leave. She had over three months accumulated. Jamie was born and she went back to work in less than a month. Most people just thought she had surgery and didn't ask questions," said Brian.

"I don't know how you managed. It must have been hard," said Maggie.

"Our neighbor, Mrs. Jarvis, kept Jamie for us. Of course, Jamie did change our lives. We arranged to pick Jamie up at six in the evening. We did communicate more. If one of us had to be away, the other one picked up Jamie. When neither of us could get Jamie, Mrs. Jarvis kept her over-night. Truth is, Jamie learned to bounce with the punches from the very beginning. We were fortunate, she was healthy and hearty," said Brian.

"She's independent for her age, that's for sure," said Maggie.

"Until you have a child you can never know how much you can love someone," said Brian. "I really love being a daddy."

"It shows," said Maggie. "When you look at Jamie you light up."

"I couldn't protect Jenny and I'm so scared I won't be able to protect Jamie," said Brian. "Protecting people is my job for heaven's sake."

"We can't always protect those we love. Life gets in the way. You're doing your best and that's all you can do," said Maggie.

"Let's get back to the car. It's beginning to get dark," said Brian.

Maggie could tell Brian was through talking. She would try not to push. They got up from the bench and began running back to the car. The traffic was gone. They were on their way.

Chapter 16

Stan found Junior in the living room watching TV. "Did you get everything unpacked and put away?" he asked.

"Didn't have much," said Junior.

"Are you excited about tomorrow?" asked Stan.

"More at nervous," said Junior. "I've been looking over these manuals. I see here that Congress passed the Narcotics Control Act in 1956 to help get rid of drug trafficking. Was that when The Farm came about?"

"No, The Farm has been around since around 1930, said Stan.

"What happened? Don't seem like we're making much headway," said Junior.

"It's a fight and will continue to be a fight as long as the suppliers keep bringing drugs in and pushing them on our young people," said Stan. "We need dedicated people like you to keep drugs under control. You'll do great in school. Just prepare the lessons and keep a low profile. At this point you don't want to make waves," said Stan. "We don't want people to know who you are or what you're really working on. Right now, I have an assignment for you. When you go to the coonhound time trials next Saturday, I have a camera I want you to take with you. It's easily concealed. It looks like a keychain. Take pictures of John Butcher, people he associates with, and anyone else you see that's suspicious," handing the camera to Junior.

"This is really something. I took a photography class once, but never had a camera like this," said Junior.

"I have another one that looks like a package of cigarettes, but you don't smoke, do you?"

"No, I've never smoked. Guess I could start if you think it would work better," said Junior.

"I think the keychain will work fine," said Stan.

"We need to build a case against the drug dealers in Durant and Boonetown," said Stan.

"Do I call you Stan or Brian? I'm a little confused," said Junior.

"Call me Brian when we're around Maggie and her parents. The only people that know my real name are you and other people that I've known for a long time," said Stan.

"Maybe I can keep it straight," said Junior. "I thought I told you, maybe I didn't, Mr. Avery entered Blue in the trials. Do you remember Blue is my dog now? Mr. Avery gave him to me when he gave us the truck."

"I can't remember, maybe you did tell me. Well, that makes it perfect. You have a dog in the competition. You'll have a good reason for being there and even a good reason for having a camera should someone notice it," said Stan.

"I know for sure there is at least one other addict in Boonetown and I know who sold me the drugs, but I want to find out who brings the drugs in," said Junior.

"You're thinking like CIA. Think big. We need to nail the top guys. Local law enforcement doesn't seem to be getting anywhere fast." said Stan. "And they are dragging their feet on Jenny's case. What time do you need to be at school in the morning?"

"Eight o'clock. Hey, I'll make eggs and toast for breakfast if you want. That way you can sleep until I call breakfast," said Junior.

"I'll be up. You have the truck, so I won't need to take you to school. I have some things at The Farm to take care of and a couple of things to check on for Jenny," said Stan. "But breakfast sounds good. I'll be ready to eat when you get it ready."

Turned out Junior wasn't a bad cook. Stan said he could get used to eating eggs for breakfast. Junior said a man needs a hardy breakfast if he's going to stay on top of his game. And stay on top of his game he did. He was soon seen as one of the brighter men in his class, although more than half the class thought he shouldn't be there because he was black. Snide remarks were often thrown his way, but Junior was determined to make a go of it. He studied until eleven o'clock every night and Stan was there to give him pointers and clarify questions. Plus, he had the advantage of working while going to school. Of course, no one knew he was already on the job, not even his teachers. His first big assignment was on Saturday.

The field trials were held just outside Durant where a long stretch of meadow was lined on both sides by a thick, green, lush forest. The trails had been prepared. Dead raccoons were dragged on the ground to create a scent for the dogs to follow. Rabbits and groundhogs were also dragged on the ground and taken in another direction from the raccoons. The dogs would be required to follow the correct scent. At the end of the hunt the dead raccoons were placed in two different trees. The first dog to 'bark up a tree' with a coon would win the event and be declared the best hunter in the bunch. The winner's owner would receive a trophy and fifty dollars. This year there was an added incentive. The winning dog would be highlighted in an advertisement on TV showing him 'barking up a tree'.

There were nineteen dogs registered and eighteen of them had arrived early. Trucks and cars were parked at the far end of the greenway. Ply lines were strung across the field with a place for each dog and a sign that read: "Please keep dogs on leash and behind the line until the starter bell sounds." Flags marked the scent lines. Six dogs were allowed to participate in each heat. Dogs were pulling at their leashes; yelps in all manner of tones filled the air. It was clear. There was a coon in the area and they were ready to catch it. Junior arrived and took his place with Blue just before the hunt was declared. Only three dogs were disqualified, one for a no show, another because his owner released him too soon and a third female appeared to be in heat, distracting the male dogs. John Butcher was there with his dog, Sam, and George Anderson was there with Ole Red. Avery was the first to arrive. He and Banjo were tense with anticipation. Some came from as far away as Alabama. The dogs were blue ticks, redbones and black and tan hounds. Robert Jones, the Pentecostal preacher, and Jim from the slaughterhouse stood near the tree line. John Butcher stood with his hound while his song writer friend stood in the crowd. The two line-judges and three tree-judges took their places. Banjo, Ole Red and four other dogs were in the first heat. The announcement began: *Gentlemen, welcome to the Field Trials of 1960. There are seven coonhound breeds and today we are showing five of these breeds, some of the finest dogs since the early settlers brought them from Europe. As you can hear, they are ready to go, so without further ado, on your mark.* The excitement caused dog and owner to tense up. "Gentlemen, it's time, 10, 9, 8, 7, 6, 5, 4, 3, 2, 1, unleash your hounds! Dogs began running in every direction, smelling the ground, yelping, howling and crying filled the air. The dogs must complete the trial and find the coon within fifteen minutes. The line-judges looked to see how well the dogs followed the scent. One of the dogs from Alabama ran outside the flags, another lost the scent and returned to his owner, but Banjo stayed on course and was the first to 'bark up the tree' where the coon was placed. Ole Red was not far behind and one of the Alabama dogs was there just before the fifteen-minute bell rang. The winners for the first heat were recorded. Dogs and owners went to the back of the field while the course was reset for the second heat.

Blue, Sam and four other dogs from Alabama and Western Kentucky were competing together. One of the Western Kentucky dogs arrived at the tree first. Blue and an Alabama dog arrived at almost the same time. The tree-judge made the decision to put Blue a few seconds ahead of the other hound.

After the track was reset, the other six hounds ran their race. Winners were recorded. Line-judges and tree-judges compared notes. The fastest and most precise trackers were declared the winners.

Over the loudspeaker came the voice of the judge: *Gentlemen, we have the winners! Gather around.* People walked closer to the stand. *Third place goes to Ole Red, owner George Anderson.* People clapped. George looked stunned. He walked forward with Ole Red to receive their ribbon. "Thank you," he said. *Second place goes to Blue, owner Junior Joseph.* Junior was standing with Blue near John Butcher and his friend. "First time a coon won the coonhound contest," said John Butcher, laughing. Junior heard him but ignored his comment and went forward to receive his ribbon. He had hoped to take some incriminating pictures, but so far had not had an opportunity. "Thank you," said Junior. "Mr. Sutton trained Blue. He deserves this ribbon."

And, for the winner! First place goes to Banjo, owner Avery Sutton. Avery stepped forward with Banjo, smiling and walking with a swagger. Even Banjo knew he was special. He seemed to stand up straighter to show off his beautiful blue tick coat. "It's an honor to be here and to share Banjo with you. He's a remarkable hunter and the best dog I've ever owned. Thank you, so much," said Avery, accepting the trophy and fifty dollars. The photographer from *The Times* newspaper took their picture. Avery and Banjo's picture would be in tomorrow's newspaper and they would be on the TV news tonight. The TV photographer had already photographed Banjo as he 'barked up the tree'.

Everyone gathered around to congratulate Avery and Banjo. John Butcher was the first. "Didn't I tell you?" he said.

"You sure did," said Avery. "You're a man that knows his dogs."

"I'll look forward to our next hunt," said John Butcher. "Will we go on Friday night?"

"I'll be ready," said Avery.

Junior hitched Blue to the back of his truck that was parked in the shade near the woods. Blue was ready for some water and a rest. As Junior was going back to the crowd, he noticed Robby Jones and Jim off to the side in the edge of the woods. He managed to circle around and watch Robby Jones helping Jim load several bags of heroin into Jim's truck. Junior took five good pictures. At least he would have something for Stan.

The Farm

It was Saturday. After lunch, Stan felt a need to go to the office. He wanted to review his information about the drug investigation. J. Morris had warned him to stay clear of Jenny's investigation. He was trying. When Jenny went missing, Stan panicked, changed Jamie's name and moved her to a different school. There was no guarantee he could keep her safe.

Stan had investigated every school and every teacher that might come into contact with Jamie. The folder with Maggie Adam's name on it lay on his desk. He picked it up and began to read:

Maggie Adams, born July 15, 1934, is the daughter of Avery (farmer) and Lucy (factory worker) Sutton from Boonetown Kentucky. She began teaching first graded at Durant Elementary School in 1958. She married Tom Adams about three months before he was shipped out to Vietnam. She resides at 2700 Main St. and runs in the neighborhood three or four times a week. There was nothing in the report about Tom dying.

"Boonetown?" thought Stan. "Junior is from Boonetown. Junior was on heroin. He knows Maggie's daddy. There's a connection. Can Maggie be trusted with my little girl?

Stan's emotions were all over the place. He couldn't imagine someone like Maggie being connected to drugs, but he knew better. He had seen worse. He would stay alert.

It was four o'clock when Stan looked up to see Junior standing in his office door.

"Hey, bud. What did you find out?" asked Stan.

"Well, not as much as I had hoped, but I did get some pictures," said Junior. "I believe I caught two men transporting heroin for resell."

"How do you know it is for resell?" asked Stan.

"There was too much of it. It looked like about seven or eight bundles, of rose/gray heroin," said Junior. "One of the guys is using a syringe. If you look close enough you can see the tracks on his arms. He's that guy, Jim, from the slaughterhouse who had the run-in with Maggie at the drugstore in Boonetown."

"Good job. I'll take this film to the lab and develop the pictures," said Stan. "Do you want to come with me?"

"No, I've got some studying to do, but one thing before I go, I don't know if you need to know this or not, Blue and me won second place at the field trial," said Junior, laughing.

"Who won first?" asked Stan.

"Mr. Sutton and Banjo, they're on tonight's news and Banjo will be on TV barking up a tree advertising the Coon Hunter's Club.

"Looks like you're getting into this coon hunting game," said Stan. "That may work to our advantage. See you in the morning. Are you making eggs?"

"Sure, be glad to," said Junior.

After Stan finished at the lab, he called Sheriff Madden. "I've got some pictures I think you'll be interested in," he said.

"Let's get together in the morning. I'll meet you at The Farm." said Sheriff Madden. "Say about 9:00 o'clock?"

Stan met with Sheriff Madden Sunday morning after the field trials and they agreed, it was worth the risk of tipping off the big man to get the drug dealers off the streets in Boonetown. The arrest would be made the following week.

Chapter 17

Aweek passed. Friday night came. The men had agreed to meet at the tree line near the edge of the Jungle. When Avery arrived, Robby Jones was waiting.

"You're early," said Avery.

"Yeah, I got things tied up a little sooner than I had expected," said Robby. "Congratulations again on your win."

"It's the best thing that ever happened to me," said Avery. "And I don't think it would have happened without John Butcher's help He's a mighty good man."

"He has his good qualities alright. I don't know if you know, but my wife and I were never able to have our own children. It was John Butcher who helped us adopt. We now have a girl and a boy, sister and brother. They are, five and six years old. We are so blessed to have them. I don't know what we'd do if we ever had to give them up," said Robby.

The roar of a truck came up behind them. It was John Butcher and his songwriter friend. John was driving. "Thought I was going to be late," said John.

"Nah, we're just chewing the fat," said Avery. "Talking about how big my head is tonight."

"Maybe Banjo'll teach us a few tricks of the trade tonight," said John.

John's friend sauntered out of the truck and came over to where Avery and Robby were talking. "How would you like to sell that show hound of yours?" he said.

"I've never thought of selling him. I'd hate awful bad to part with him," said Avery, as George Anderson joined the group.

"There ain't enough money in Montgomery County to buy that dog," said George.

"Would you take a hundred dollars?" asked the songwriter.

"Can't part with him," said Avery.

As Avery and the songwriter were joking around about selling Banjo, Robby and John had gone on the other side of the truck. "Did you get it?" asked John.

"It's in the back of my truck," said Robby.

"You take Avery and George toward the woods and we'll transfer it to my truck," said John.

"Let's let the dogs go," said Robby. "I need to get home early tonight."

"Come on Banjo," said Avery, as he headed toward the Jungle. Banjo immediately picked up a scent and headed into the brush. Avery and George followed. The others lingered back.

"This is the last time," said Robby. "I can't put my family in danger."

"If you don't do it, you may not have a family," said John.

"I can't believe you would do that to me," said Robby.

"That and more," said John.

"Please don't," said Robby.

"Stop your sniveling. You knew what you were getting into when you agreed to our deal. Now keep up your end and keep your mouth shut," said John, as they transferred the drugs into John Butcher' truck.

"I need to go," said Robby, as he went to the edge of the woods to call his dog. "Tell Avery I'm not feeling so good."

Robby went straight home from the hunt. He didn't lie. He wasn't feeling well and he was about to feel worse. The sheriff was waiting for him.

"Good evening, Sheriff Madden. What brings you my way tonight?" asked Robby.

"Reverend Robert Jones?"

"Yes, Sheriff you know who I am," said Robby.

"I have a warrant for your arrest for peddling drugs. Turn around so I can cuff you," said Sheriff Madden.

"Before you cuff me and take me in, can I go kiss my children goodnight and tell my wife I love her?" asked Robby. "There's no way I'll be able to explain this."

"Yeah, go on," said the sheriff. He had known Robby for over fifteen years and just hated he had gotten himself into such a mess. Deep down the sheriff knew something had gone mightily wrong.

Robby went in the house to tell his children goodnight and tell his wife what was happening while the sheriff waited in his car. Robby's wife knew John Butcher had gone the extra mile to help them with their adoption, but she was unaware of the pressure Robby had been under, and there was nothing left to be said. The pieces would fall where they would. There was nothing he could do about it. After ten minutes Robby came back outside. "I'm ready to go," he said.

Prosecutor, J. Morris Higgins, told Stan the boys were caught red handed and pleaded guilty. When Sheriff Madden was arresting Robert Jones, the sheriff's deputy was arresting Jim. Jim had some of the unsold heroin in his possession. Both men were taken to jail in Durant.

Robby was sent to The Farm for three months and Jim received a six-month sentence. The photographs were used as evidence. There was no need for witnesses.

Chapter 18

B rian called Maggie. "I hear your daddy and his dog, Banjo, won the field trial," said Brian.

"Yeah, how did you find out?"

"Junior told me. He entered his dog and he won second place."

"Daddy's beaming. I tried to get up enough courage to warn him about the kind of man John Butcher is, but I just couldn't ruin his day," said Maggie. "I bet Junior was excited. Tell him congratulations for me."

"He's not into hunting that much, but Junior was proud for your daddy because he was the one who trained his dog," said Brian.

"To change the subject, I've sent Jamie's test to be scored. I'm sure she did well. I can't believe I won't see her until school starts back. Are you going to Missouri anytime soon?"

"I try to go every other week. Do you want to go next time?" asked Brian.

"Yes, definitely, just let me know when," said Maggie. "I got her some more little people for her surprise. Does she like cats or dogs? I couldn't decide so I got both."

"I think she likes both. We've never had an animal. We're too mobile to take care of one," said Brian. "There's something going down in Boonetown tonight so it will be next Friday before I can go to see Jamie. I'll come over after the arrests are made and tell you about it."

"Daddy is so innocent. He sees good in everyone," said Maggie. "I wish there was some way I could protect him."

"In your own words, we can't always protect the people we love," said Brian.

"I know," said Maggie.

Maggie called her daddy. "I just called to say I love you," she said. How are you?"

"I'm alright I guess," said Avery.

"I hear a little dread in your voice," said Maggie. "What's wrong?"

"Some of the boys are into drugs," said Avery. It's all over town. People are talking. They've been arrested. I hope Junior's not into drugs again."

"I see Junior quite often and he's doing fine," said Maggie.

"I just can't understand why anyone would get mixed up with drugs," said Avery.

"It's sad," said Maggie. "Maybe The Farm will straighten your friends out. I wish things were different."

"Maybe so," said Avery, his voice low and choked. "If this keeps up, I won't have anybody to go hunting with except John Butcher."

Maggie didn't hear from Brian until Wednesday after the arrest. "Can I come over?" he asked. "I'll stop by the meat and three and bring dinner."

"Sounds good to me," said Maggie, wishing she had washed her hair the night before.

Brian picked up chicken, corn and green beans. Corn bread and iced tea were included. He came in and put the meals on the table.

"Drug arrests have been made and you won't believe who was arrested," said Brian.

"Let me guess. Junior told us Jim is using, so Jim for one. And I don't know who the other one is," said Maggie.

"The Reverend Robert Jones, the Pentecostal pastor," said Brian.

"Oh, I think Daddy knows him. He goes hunting with the guys. Daddy told me some of the boys were arrested. He was worried about Junior," said Maggie.

As Maggie and Brian ate their dinner, they made plans for Friday night to go to Missouri. This time they would spend the night.

Maggie was no longer in school so she told Brian she could leave anytime he was ready. At four o'clock in the afternoon Brian called. "My car is acting up. I think it needs a break job and maybe an oil change. We may have to postpone our trip."

"No, Jamie is expecting us. I'll drive my car," said Maggie. "A Camaro is not big and fine like your Lincoln, but it'll get us there." Maggie's Camaro was sporty—black with a silver stripe and chrome spoked hubcaps. It had belonged to Tom. The car was one of the things that attracted Maggie to him.

"I don't want to put you out," said Brian.

"You're not putting me out. My car was serviced last week and it's full of gas and ready to go. I'll pick you up in thirty minutes. Where do you live?" said Maggie.

"I don't give my address to everyone," said Brian, laughing. "But, if you're going to pick me up, I guess I have to. It's 327 Taylor Street."

"Is that over close to the meat and three?" asked Maggie.

"Second street over from there," said Brian.

"See you in a bit," said Maggie.

Maggie turned on to Taylor Street. The houses were small, mostly two bedrooms. She counted the numbers—326. There on the left was 327. Brian was waiting in the driveway. As soon as Maggie stopped the car, he opened the door and got in. "You didn't have any trouble finding me?" asked Brian.

"No, it was pretty easy," said Maggie, as she backed out of the driveway.

When Maggie and Brian turned on to Highway 60 it was beginning to rain. The sun had set and the rain made it seem darker than usual. The on-coming headlights were blinding.

"Slow down," said Brian. "This road can be slippery."

"Don't worry, this Camaro has good traction in wet weather," said Maggie, just as a pickup truck came around the curve on the wrong side of the road, side swiping the Camaro on the driver's side forcing Maggie off the road. She was slumped over the steering wheel. Brian jumped out of the car and ran around to the driver's side. He yanked at the door but was unable to open it. He took a hammer tool he always carried in his pocket and broke the window, reached in and unlocked the door.

"Maggie, Maggie can you hear me?" said Brian, softly rubbing Maggie's forehead. Maggie was unconscious. Brian was accustomed to having all his equipment in his car. He didn't even have a phone. He stopped the next car. "Please call an ambulance. My friend and the driver of the pickup are hurt," he said. He sat with Maggie holding her hand, talking to her. It was ten minutes before he heard the sirens. Brian breathed a sigh. The attendants loaded Maggie into the ambulance, just as she was beginning to open her eyes. The driver of the pickup said he was ok, a skinned arm and a knot on his head was all. He refused to go to the hospital. The highway patrol answered the call and took down the car tags and accident information. Brian gave them Maggie's address and phone number and he took the name and number of the man who was driving the truck. Brian looked at the EMT, "I think our car will drive. I'll follow you," said Brian. They pulled out together headed toward Durant General Hospital. His knee was swollen and hurting. His sock was bloody. There was a small cut on his leg. He had not noticed until now.

Brian sat in the emergency room waiting area. "Can I go back to be with Maggie?" he asked the attendant.

"Are you family?"

"No, but family lives in another town and she needs someone with her," said Brian.

"She's talking. I'll ask her if you can come back," said the nurse.

Maggie said Brian could come back to her room. She was glad to see him. "What happened?" she asked.

"That man in a pickup truck came around the corner on your side of the road. He was driving too fast and didn't make the corner. He may have been drinking or on drugs. He refused to get examined and wouldn't come to the hospital," said Brian. "How are you feeling?"

"The doctor said I have a concussion. They'll keep me overnight. Guess I'm going to have a heck of a headache," said Maggie.

"You scared me. I'm glad you're going to be alright," said Brian. "I need to find a phone and call mother. She'll be looking for us to arrive about now." Brian went to find a pay phone. As soon as he finished talking to his mother and Jamie he hurried back to Maggie's room.

"Do you want me to call your parents?" asked Brian.

"No, they would think they'd need to come down here and I don't want them driving at night in the rain," said Maggie. "I'll be alright."

"I'll make sure of that. I'm not going anywhere," said Brian. "I'll call your daddy in the morning. You close your eyes and rest. I'll be right here if you need anything." Brian stretched out on the lounge chair and picked up a newspaper that was left in the room. There it was in large type: **Boonetown Man Wins Coonhound Field Trials.** Right there on the front page was a picture of Maggie's daddy and Banjo. He would make sure to save the paper for Maggie.

He drifted off to sleep and the next thing he knew Maggie was saying his name: "Brian, are you still here?"

"Yes, I'm here. Can I get you something?" asked Brian.

"Do you think I can have some water?" asked Maggie.

"I'll see," said Brian, as he rang the bell.

"Yes?"

"Can Maggie have water?" asked Brian.

"I'll bring her some," said the nurse. The nurse came in with a fresh pitcher of water. "Just sip it," she said.

"What time is it?" asked Maggie.

"Two in the morning," said Brian. He thought how natural it felt to be with Maggie at two in the morning. How he wanted to be near her. How he had panicked over the thought of her being hurt. How he never wanted to leave her side again. But he couldn't tell her. It was too soon. It had only been seven months since both had lost their partners. Seven months had seemed like an eternity to him. Jenny's murder was still unsolved, and he was about to get into a full-blown drug trafficking case. The time was not right.

Maggie slept peacefully until seven a.m. when she turned over and looked at Brian.

"Good morning, sunshine," said Brian.

"Did you spend the night?" asked Maggie.

"Yes, you didn't think I'd leave you here by yourself, did you?"

"Thank you for staying. I need to let Daddy and Mother know I'm in the hospital or they'll be fuming mad at me," said Maggie. "Oh, my head hurts."

"If you think you'll be alright I'll go call them and see about taking your car to a body shop. Do you have a preference?" asked Brian. "I've got to take my car in, too. I'll get a loaner and come back. Maybe they'll let you go home this afternoon if you're doing well."

"That body shop over by the school seems like a nice place," said Maggie.

"I know them," said Brian. I'll take your car there and call your parents. What's their number?"

Maggie scribbled her parent's number on a napkin she found on the bedside table and handed it to Brian.

"I'll be back as soon as I can," said Brian. He found a phone booth in the hospital lobby and rang the Sutton's number.

"Hello, Mr. Sutton," said Brian. "This is Brian Scott.

"Who?" said Avery.

"I'm Maggie's friend. We were on our way to Missouri last night in Maggie's car and had a little run-in," said Brian.

"Run-in? Is Maggie alright? Do we need to come?"

"Maggie bumped her head and has spent the night in the hospital. She's going to be fine. They just wanted to keep her for observation. I think she'll go home this afternoon. I'm taking her car to a body shop as soon as I get off the phone."

"You say she's, ok?" said Avery.

"Well, they haven't released her yet, but everything looks like they'll release her this afternoon," said Brian.

"I'm not feeling too good. If she's alright, I'll wait and come tomorrow. Tell her I love her."

"Yes sir. I'll make sure she gets home and is alright before I leave and I'll tell her you said you love her," said Brian. "I hope you get to feeling better."

Brian ran his errands and returned to the hospital. "Did they say you can go?" he asked.

"Yes, as soon as the paperwork is completed. When did the body shop say my car'll be ready?" asked Maggie.

"They have to order a new door. It'll be the end of the week, but my car'll be ready on Monday. We can just switch the loaner to you after I get mine back," said Brian.

"I don't know what I'd do without you," said Maggie, half laughing, but in her heart she knew she meant every word. It was comforting to know Brian was watching out for her. She loved having him near and he didn't even seem to notice she had uncombed hair and no make-up. She didn't dare look in the mirror.

Brian told her about her daddy not feeling well. She couldn't imagine what was bothering him. He was always so healthy, always had things under control. Maybe she would find out if he decided to come to see her when she got home. He might be coming down with the flu or something. She wanted him to come, but she really didn't need him. Brian was there.

Brian brought Maggie home on Saturday night about 6:00 in the evening. Maggie said she wasn't all that hungry. She still had a bit of a headache. Brian opened a can of soup and made a grilled cheese sandwich. He said that was about the extent of his cooking. Maggie said it was just what she needed. Brian called the Suttons to let them know Maggie was home. Lucy answered the phone:

"Can I talk to Maggie?" she asked.

"Maggie, your mother wants to talk to you," said Brian.

"Hello Mother. How are you?" asked Maggie.

"I'm alright, how are you?" asked Lucy.

"I'll be alright. I've got a little headache," said Maggie.

"I'm worried about your daddy. He's just not acting right," said Lucy.

"Is he there? Let me speak to him," said Maggie.

"He's asleep. We're planning on coming down there tomorrow morning. He said he thought it would be good if I would drive," said Lucy. "Is that odd?"

"That doesn't sound like Daddy. Call me if you need me before tomorrow. I don't know what to think," said Maggie, as she hung up the phone. Now she was worried. She knew her mother had the habit of going a little overboard, but her daddy had mentioned to Brian that he wasn't feeling well. Something was going on and she didn't have a clue what.

Turning to Brian, "I'm feeling better. You can go if you want to. I guess your nosey neighbors and Junior are wondering where you are," said Maggie.

"I think I will. I need to check in with Junior. I'll call you first thing in the morning," said Brian, looking at Maggie, hesitating. "Is it ok if I kiss you goodbye?"

"Sure," said Maggie, playfully handing Brian her hand. He kissed her hand and held it with both his hands to his lips in a passionate caress. "Be safe," he said, as he left.

Chapter 19

Maggie had a restless night. First thinking about Brian and then thinking about her daddy. Did Brian really want to kiss me, bad breath, rat-hair and paleface? Is Daddy getting sick or is there something on his mind worrying him? She had seen her daddy worry and it almost always made him sick. He didn't handle stress well. Although she thought she slept only two hours, to her amazement it was 8:00 a.m. when she awoke. She slowly got out of bed and went to the shower. It felt good to wash her hair. Her headache was almost gone.

It was nearly ten when her parents knocked on the door.

"Come in," Maggie called.

They opened the door and entered the room. Avery was pale and slow to speak, but gave Maggie a little hug. "Are you alright?" he asked.

"I'm ok," said Maggie. "I still have a slight headache, but the doctor said by tomorrow I should be fine."

Avery's countenance was sad, leading Maggie to think he was worried about something.

"You know I had to drive all the way down here because your daddy wouldn't drive," said Lucy.

"You like to drive, don't you?" said Maggie.

"Yeah, but my back is killing me. It's too much when I have to do everything," said Lucy.

"Come over here and stretch out in my recliner," said Maggie. "Maybe it'll help your back."

"Ok," said Lucy, as she stretched out and Maggie turned on the TV.

"Daddy, come outside and let me show you my loaner car," said Maggie. Avery and Maggie slowly moved to the front driveway. "Now Daddy, what's got you so upset?" asked Maggie.

"First of all, I just don't know what to do about it," began Avery. "It's not something I need to be talking about. But I guess I can tell you. You can't tell anyone. You never know who you're talking to. Promise you won't tell?"

"You know I won't tell if you don't want me to," said Maggie.

"Well, I heard this airplane flying real low back over the hill behind our house. I went outside and watched and I saw something floating down from the plane. It was just back of Ole Baldy on my side of the fence, near the Jungle. I went back there and discovered something I wish I hadn't."

"What did you find?"

"You can't tell anyone about this. These fellows that deal in dope are dangerous," said Avery.

"You mean it was drugs?" asked Maggie.

"It was a whole crate of dope. I'm not sure what kind. I don't know much about dope. But, that's how the dope's getting into Boonetown," said Avery.

"I can see why you're worried," said Maggie. "I agree. I don't think we should tell anyone. I don't know what you can do about it. It could be dangerous to talk about it. I'm sure the authorities will eventually catch the big guys."

"Maybe that preacher Jones fellow will tell them what he knows, or Jim. Jim could tell. I'm sure the two of them know more than they're telling. They have to know who sold it to them," said Avery.

"It has nothing to do with you. You just need to let it alone. Don't worry. Stress is not good for you," said Maggie.

"I know, I haven't been feeling very good and a couple days ago I had a little spell down at the barn," said Avery.

"What kind of spell?" asked Maggie.

"Well, my chest and arm were hurting and I had trouble breathing," said Avery.

"What did you do?" asked Maggie.

"I came to the house and took a swig of my Kentucky Bourbon. I reckon it's pretty much good for what ails you," said Avery, laughing.

"I don't think that sounds good, and nothing to laugh about. You need to go to the doctor," said Maggie.

"They'll be wanting to put me in the hospital and I don't think I'm going to do that," said Avery. "I guess it wouldn't hurt to talk to that retired doctor that lives in town. I'll drop by his place first thing in the morning. I don't think it's anything, probably just something I ate."

"Just the same it'll make me feel better if you get checked out," said Maggie.

Lucy was standing in the door. "My program has gone off. What's taking you so long? One car looks the same as another one. We should get started back home. I don't want to take all day. I've got to get the washing done before I go back to work tomorrow." Lucy had worked for the local shirt factory for the past fifteen years. She had worked her way up to inspector and was proud of her job.

"You're right. We probably need to get going," said Avery. "Are you sure you're ok?"

"I'm fine," said Maggie. "You be careful and call me after you see the doctor."

"Do you still want me to drive?" asked Lucy.

"I think you had better," said Avery.

Maggie was on the front porch waving when she heard the phone ringing. Brian had said he would call. Maybe it was him. She ran inside and answered. "Hello, Maggie speaking," she said.

"Hello, sunshine," said Brian. "You sound like you're feeling better."

"Yep, feeling better," said Maggie. "What're you doing today?"

"I've got a few things to take care of at The Farm, but other than that, I'm free," said Brian.

"Can you come over this afternoon? I have something I think you need to know," said Maggie.

"I'll be over around two or three. How does that sound?"

"See you then," said Maggie, hanging up to go make herself another grilled cheese sandwich. She ate her sandwich slow while thinking of Brian kissing and holding her hand. Her heart was racing. She was excited about him coming over. She knew the information she had would be useful, but was conflicted about betraying her daddy's confidence.

Chapter 20

Brian arrived at 3:00 o'clock. Maggie had straightened up the house and freshened her make-up. Her freshly washed black hair gleamed, hung down around her shoulders and smelled like coconut. She had even given her nails a new coat of hot pink polish.

Brian sat down on the sofa. He was dressed in light brown pants and a blue short-sleeved shirt that showed off his tanned biceps and accented his deep blue eyes. His dark brown hair showed a bit of temple gray. There was a sober look of wonder on his face. "Did you say you have something to tell me?" he asked.

"Yes, but you have to promise you will not get my daddy involved in this drug mess," said Maggie. "No one can know he was the one who told. He doesn't know I'm telling you."

"How's your daddy involved?" asked Brian.

"He saw something," said Maggie.

"What did he see?" asked Brian, standing and walking over to the window.

"There's this hill that the country people call Ole Baldy. The Jungle where Daddy and his friends go coon hunting is right behind that hill. You can see all this from my daddy's back porch. He heard an airplane flying really low. He went out to investigate and saw the plane near the Jungle drop something. He wondered what it was so he decided to walk back there and take a look. He said it was a crate half busted open. He pried the lid off and found small packages of white powder. He thinks it's some kind of drugs. The stress is tearing him up. He's afraid and now I'm afraid. Is there anything we can do to stop these guys?" asked Maggie.

"I need to get a good look at the area," said Brian. "It won't be dark for another four hours. Let's take a ride over to Boonetown and you can show me where it happened."

"I can't let Daddy see me. He must never know I told," said Maggie. "I showed Daddy the loaner car, so we can't use it."

"Oh, didn't you notice. I have my car. They made a special effort to get it back to me early," said Brian. "But this big old Lincoln may look suspicious in Boonetown. I'll make a call and get a pickup truck for the day."

"You can do that?" asked Maggie.

"Oh, yes. We have all kinds of vehicles for official business at our disposal," said Brian. After arranging for and picking up the truck, Maggie and Brian headed to Boonetown. It was a beautiful drive. The sun was shining and a nice breeze was blowing. It was the second day of summer, but it still felt like spring.

"There are at least four ways of entering the area," said Maggie. "You can come in from the north on Highway 60 toward the Jungle or you can come in from the south on Highway 80. Smaller roads lead to the Jungle or to my daddy's house. One of the roads goes over the hills toward the mountain out past where George and Martha Anderson live. I guess you know that area well."

"This is a perfect location for bringing the narcotics in. There are all kinds of escape routes and there's a small airport about ten miles from Boonetown where the plane can refuel. Did your daddy say what kind of plane it was that dropped the drugs?" asked Brian.

"No, I don't think he would know that. He said it was a small plane," said Maggie.

"Probably a two or three-seater," said Brian. "If it was just the pilot there would be enough room for several crates. He kicks it out as he goes. Once the plane is empty, the pilot refuels and heads back for more. It's a pretty common practice."

"Then Daddy has stumbled upon something significant?" asked Maggie.

"I'd say your daddy has provided us with a big piece of the puzzle," said Brian.

"Turn here," said Maggie, as they turned down the road where she was raised. "This is my old stomping ground. See the reason they call that hill Ole Baldy?"

"Yeah, it's as bald as an old man's head, no trees at all," said Brian. "How do we get to the Jungle?"

"Two ways. You can turn around and go back through Boonetown and head north, or you can go on past our house and over the big tall hill and circle back around. It's not far either way," said Maggie. There was nobody outside at her parent's house. The car was sitting in the driveway, a small light shown in the bedroom window. Brian drove past the Sutton house and over the hill. The hill was the highest point before the mountain. You could see for miles. Brian stopped the truck and killed the motor. "This reminds me of when I was a teenager." he said, reaching for Maggie's hand. "Some of us would take our girls to what we called lookout point to make out." Maggie moved closer to Brian and laid her head on his shoulder. They sat silent, taking in the scenery. Then Brian reached down and took her chin in his hand, bringing his lips to touch hers. The sun was setting. Brilliant colors of orange, pink, blue and green laced the landscape as dusk crept in and the sun dropped below the horizon.

Brian turned on the truck headlights and drove around to the clearing at the tree line of the Jungle. "This is where the hunters meet to go hunting," said Maggie.

"It's ideal for the drug traffickers," said Brian. "They can drive close to the drop and pick it up without being noticed. Are there any houses near here?"

"Not for two or three miles," said Maggie. "I went hunting in the Jungle with Daddy once. I was about thirteen years old. The Jungle is a scary place. It's dark and wild animals are everywhere. I guess that's why it's a good place to train the coonhounds."

"We'll have to come back some day and go in there," said Brian. "But, right now I want to get back to Durant. I want to talk to Junior. I think I have a job for him. About the kiss. . .".

"Did you mean it when you said you took 'your girl' to Lookout Point? Since we kissed at Lookout Point, does that mean, I'm your girl?" asked Maggie.

"I would be so happy if you would be my girl if I'm not acting too soon. I don't want to rush you," said Brian.

"I only know what I feel and I want to be near you. You make me happy and I would be honored to be your girl, but what about you. You're still grieving," said Maggie.

"For the past seven months we've grieved together. I'll honor Jenny's memory, but I'm ready to solve her case. Maybe by the end of the summer we can have some closure. I love being with you," said Brian, as he reached over and kissed Maggie on the cheek.

They drove back to Durant in silence listening to the jazz station on the radio. Miles Davis maneuvered the classic melody of *Kind of Blue* with mesmerizing precision.

When Brian arrived home, he wanted to talk to Junior, but Junior was already in bed and sound asleep. He would have to wait until morning.

Brian thought about the kiss. The wanted to talk to Maggie. His heart began to beat faster as he rang her number.

"Hi, I just wanted to say good night," said Brian.

"I'm in bed. Ella Fitzgerald is singing, *For Once in My Life.* I don't think I've ever been this happy," said Maggie.

"The feeling is mutual," said Brian. "Maybe I'll put on some jazz, too. I need something to drown out the investigation. I'll call you tomorrow. Good night, sleep tight."

"Good night," said Maggie. She hoped she would dream about Brian.

Brian listened to Jazz as he fell asleep. He awoke early and was waiting for Junior when he came out of his bedroom. "Good morning. How did you sleep?" asked Brian.

"I must have slept sound. I didn't hear you come in," said Junior, dressing on the way to the door. "I'm late for school. I have to go."

"Here, eat this apple on the way," said Brian. "Come by my office after school. I'm meeting with Jenny's lawyer today to go over her will and tell him what's happening with the drug case. We don't have much on Jenny's murder case, but things are inching along. Maybe her lawyer will have some ideas as to how to proceed."

Running out the door, "See you after school," said Junior.

Brian made himself a peanut butter and jelly sandwich. Poured a large glass of milk and swigged it down. Thoughts of Maggie troubled his mind. He wondered if she liked peanut butter and jelly, if she drank milk or coffee for breakfast, maybe juice. There was so much to learn about her and he found himself wanting to know everything, even though he knew he was not being honest with her.

After eating his sandwich, Brian picked up the phone and dialed Maggie's number.

"Hello," said Maggie.

Ella still singing this morning?" asked Brian.

"No, I turned her off sometime during the night when the grinding on the turntable woke me up. I went to sleep listening to her. I hadn't done that since I was a teenager," said Maggie.

"I love to listen to music in my sleep," said Brian. "It drowns out work. I was thinking last night during the night, we should keep our relationship a secret until the trial is over. I don't want you to have anything to do with the investigation. Your daddy is right. These dope guys are dangerous."

"Do you think the dope dealers and Jenny's case are connected?" asked Maggie.

"We don't have any proof. I can't really talk to you about that. I want to keep you out of it," said Brian.

"As long as we can see each other I'll be fine," said Maggie.

"There may be times when we'll have to stay apart. We'll take it as it comes," said Brian.

"I'm going to check on Daddy later today. Call me tonight," said Maggie.

"I will," said Brian, as he headed for the shower. He had an appointment with J. Morris Higgins at 10:30.

The Farm

Stan met with his friend and lawyer. They first talked about Jenny's will. She had left everything she had to Jamie except a thousand dollars would go to her parents to make repairs and put indoor plumbing in their house. Her bank account was fifteen thousand dollars and some change. She must have saved almost all of her earnings. Stan knew she was frugal, but never knew how frugal. There was little else. The house was in Stan's alias James Therman's name and the furniture was mostly hand-me-downs from thrift stores. Stan was appointed the conservator of Jamie's estate, and he would certainly manage her money well, saving it for her education. After the will was read, Stan and J. Morris turned their thoughts to the drug problem.

"We're beginning to get somewhere," said Stan. "We may know how the drugs are being transported into this area. We're investigating this week."

"Make me a list of potential witnesses for Jenny's case," said J. Morris. "We have that fingerprint, but little else. It's been a long time. I guess the guy thinks he's gotten away with it, but no matter how long it takes we'll get him."

"Keep me posted," said Stan, as they parted ways.

Stan stopped by the meat and three to grab a bite of lunch before he went back to The Farm to talk to Robby Jones and Jim. He was hoping to get them to tell him who their supplier was. The question now was, if they were in jail, who was picking the drugs up and who was disbursing them on the street? There must be at least one other person in Boonetown or close by Boonetown who was in the drug business.

At five o'clock Junior stuck his head in the office door. "Did you need to talk to me?" he asked.

"Yeah, I found out something you need to know," said Stan. "I have reason to believe the drugs in this area are being brought in by a small airplane. I think the plane is refueling at Westfield Airport."

"You mean that little airport that's half-way between here and Boonetown?"

"That's the one," said Stan.

"We have a cleaning crew operating out of that airport. On Friday night I'll arrange for you to replace one of the crew members. There are certain things I want you to come away with," said Stan.

"Ok, sounds interesting," said Junior.

"I need to know what kind of plane is refueling around 5:30 to 6:30 at night. I would love to have a copy of the flight plan. If you can get a good look at the pilot, I'll need a description. And on top of all that you will have to do a good job cleaning. The airport authorities don't know we're investigating."

"I understand," said Junior, as he left for home.

Chapter 21

Maggie was troubled and wondering about her daddy. It was too early to call. She would have to wait until at least midafternoon before she would know what the doctor told her daddy about his 'little spell'. She had a feeling her daddy was downplaying the 'spell'. He refused to drive. She was sure it was more than he was telling. She busied herself with making a summer activity box for Jamie. If she couldn't go see her, she could at least stay in touch. The IQ test would be back the third week of July. She was excited to find out how her students placed. The test results would be stored in the principal's office until teacher in-service day. She had checked Jamie's test and already knew she had scored high.

It was after twelve. Maggie was about to call her daddy when the phone rang. "Maggie," said her daddy. "Dr. Pearl said he's pretty sure it's my heart."

"Your heart? How bad is it?" asked Maggie.

"The doctor wants me to have a procedure where they put dye into my veins and take an x-ray to see if any of my veins are blocked. He has made an appointment for me tomorrow at Durant General," said Avery. "Do you think you can go with me? Your mother said she has to work."

"You know I will. I'll come and get you. You don't need to be driving," said Maggie. "What time is your appointment?"

"One o'clock, said to be there around eleven," said Avery.

"I'll be there at eight to pick you up. Don't do much between now and then. Take it easy," said Maggie.

"I'll try to. I'll need to get somebody to feed the cows for me," said Avery. "Right now, I need to lie down."

After talking to her daddy, Maggie sat down on the couch, when the phone rang again. It was Brian. "I've decided to go see Jamie early tomorrow. Do you want to go?"

"I can't," said Maggie. "I just heard from Daddy. He's having an arteriogram tomorrow. I'll have to go get him and bring him down here. He's scared. He's never been in a hospital before. I'm so sorry. I really want to see Jamie. Come over and get the activity box I made for her and tell her I love her," said Maggie. "Tell her I promise I'll come next time."

"I'll pick the box up soon if that's alright. I need to go see Martha and George. Jenny left them some money to put plumbing in their house. It sounds like a good idea, but George might just throw a fit and say he doesn't want it. Country people like for things to stay the same," said Brian.

"I can understand where he's coming from," said Maggie. "I'll look forward to seeing you.

Brian went to see Maggie on his way to Pilot Ridge. She had the box assembled for him and when he was ready to leave, he held her close and kissed her goodbye.

"Jamie is talking of coming back to Durant for school. I hope to have things under control by September when school starts back," said Brian. "I checked. It'll be the Monday after Labor Day."

"If her test scores are as good as I think they'll be, she'll easily advance to third grade," said Maggie.

Brian arrived back in Durant on Sunday morning. When he put the key in the lock, he heard the phone ringing. Maggie was calling.

"Hello, glad you're back. How was Jamie?"

"Jamie is fine, gnawing at the bit to get back to Durant. I really hope she can come back to school next year," said Brian.

"I do, too. I really miss her. Did she ask about me?"

"She wanted to know why you didn't come. I told her your daddy is sick and she understood," said Brian. "How is he?"

"He needs bypass surgery. The doctor wanted to take him straight to surgery, but Daddy said he had to come home to arrange for the neighbors to take care of his animals before he can go in the hospital. I know he's scared. I came home with him. His surgery is scheduled for Monday. I'm going to try to talk him into coming to Durant today to make it easier tomorrow," said Maggie.

"That's a serious surgery. How old is your daddy?" asked Brian.

"He's fifty-six. The doctor said he has to have it. Without the surgery he'll have a major heart attack soon. As a matter of fact, the doctor said he might have one before he gets back in the hospital. That's the reason I came home with him. Mother is trying to decide if she is coming to Durant or working. I think she needs to come to the hospital. Daddy needs all the support he can get," said Maggie.

"This is terrible timing. I wish I could be with you, but I've got information I have to follow up on. I'll be out of town for a couple of days," said Brian.

"I understand. Hopefully we'll be out of the hospital when you get back. If not and all goes well, we'll be in Durant General. I'll stay with him. Mother wouldn't be able to handle it by herself," said Maggie.

"I'm leaving tonight. I'll drive most of the night and get a motel room tomorrow morning. I have a few places where I can gather information. I think we're on to something. I'll see you when I get back," said Brian.

"Be careful," said Maggie.

"Always," said Brian, as they said good-bye.

Maggie turned to her daddy. "Why don't we go to Durant this afternoon so we'll be close to the hospital in the morning? It'll make things easier," she said.

"I think that's a good idea," said Avery. He had never before agreed to spend the night at Maggie's house. He had rarely ever spent the night away from home. He must have felt something or else he was taking the doctor's words seriously. When he left the hospital, the doctor said he did not recommend him leaving the hospital. Lucy came to Maggie's house with Avery. She said she had some vacation time that she could take so that her job would still be there when she got back. Her employer didn't take laying out of work lightly, but Maggie told her Avery needed her and the shirt factory would just have to understand.

It was almost five o'clock in the evening when they arrived at Maggie's house. Maggie fixed hamburgers and fried potatoes. Avery didn't eat very much. He wouldn't be allowed to eat breakfast. He mostly sat silent in front of the TV. Lucy talked and talked. *The woman who works on the machine next to her wears the strangest clothes and she must never take a bath. She always smells funny. The woman on the other side of her had surgery. Is took her a long time to heal.* Maggie pretended to listen, but had her mind on other things. *What if Daddy doesn't make it through the surgery? What if Brian is doing something dangerous?*

"Yes, Mother everything's going to be alright. Durant General is known for heart surgery and Daddy's doctor is one of the best heart surgeons. We'll be there with him to give him encouragement. Make sure to take a change of clothes in your bag. We'll probably be at the hospital for at least a week," said Maggie, trying to act like it was just a matter-of-fact.

Lucy and Avery went to bed early in the spare bedroom. Maggie finished cleaning up the kitchen and retired to her bedroom. *Brian, Brian, where are you?* She knew he was still on the road. She hoped he was being careful. She went to sleep thinking about him.

"Maggie, Maggie come quick," said Lucy. "There's something wrong with your daddy."

Maggie jumped out of bed and ran to the spare bedroom. Avery was unable to speak. He clutched his chest. His mouth was open and his eyes set. Maggie ran for the phone to call the operator. "Send me an ambulance to twenty-seven hundred Main Street. My daddy is having a heart attack," said Maggie, running back to her daddy's side. Maggie began chest compressions and mouth to mouth resuscitation.

"Stop, you're hurting him," shouted Lucy, trying to kiss and love on Avery.

"Move mother. I need room," said Maggie, looking at the clock. It had been five minutes. Where was the ambulance? Then she heard the siren on the huge Cadillac hearse pulling into her driveway. She ran to the door. "In here," she said.

The attendants rushed in and began CPR and oxygen on Avery as they loaded him into the hearse. "Take him to Durant General. He's due for heart surgery tomorrow," said Maggie. "His doctor's name is Kenneth Freeman. Mother and I will follow you in my car."

Just as Maggie and Lucy arrived in the emergency room, Doctor Freeman came running through. He stopped to talk. "We're prepping him for surgery, now. You can wait in the cardio waiting room. A nurse will give you updates. The surgery should take around four hours. I have to tell you. He may not make it. He's not in good shape."

Lucy sat crying and wringing her hands. Maggie was trying to stay calm. "Mother, do you want a cup of coffee?" she asked.

"How can you think of eating at a time like this?" said Lucy. "Lord, don't let him die," she prayed.

Maggie poured herself a cup of coffee and tried to sit down with a magazine. Lucy was up walking the floor.

"Mother, we have four hours to wait. We need to stay calm," said Maggie.

"You can't stay calm when your husband is dying. He's your daddy. You don't care. Don't you know if he dies, I'll be left alone?" Maggie knew it wouldn't do any good to try to talk her mother down. She would just continue to rave, so she sat in a chair across the room and looked out the window. It was beginning to get daylight when she looked up to see the Reverend Robby Jones coming into the room. He walked over to shake hands with Lucy.

"How is he?" he asked.

"They're operating now. I don't think he's going to make it. The doctor said his chances are slim," said Lucy.

Maggie came over to where the preacher and Lucy were sitting. She extended her hand. "I'm Maggie Adams, Avery's daughter," she said.

"I'm Robby Jones. I'm the preacher at the Pentecostal Church in Boonetown. I hunt some with your daddy," said Robby Jones.

"Oh," said Maggie. "I thought you were spending some time at The Farm."

"Yes, I was, but I got early release. My parole officer gave me permission to come to the hospital to be with one of my parishioners."

"He just went into surgery," said Maggie.

"You say, he's in trouble? Is it alright if we have prayer?" said Reverend Jones.

"Yes, I guess so," said Maggie.

Reverend Jones began praying entreating the Lord to save Avery's life. Maggie and Lucy sat with their eyes closed hanging on to his every word.

A nurse entered the room and sat down in front of Lucy. "Mrs. Sutton, your husband is holding his own. He's in critical condition and we still don't know if he'll survive the surgery. But for now, he's still alive. We have about two more hours of surgery. I'll check back."

Reverend Jones reached and held Lucy's hand. "Thank you, Lord for this good report. Thank you for allowing Mr. Avery to survive this far and we pray for your continued sustaining power. Amen."

"Thank you for coming," said Maggie. "How did you know Daddy was in the hospital?"

"I was here because one of our deacons is sick. I just happened to see Mr. Sutton brought in to the emergency room and asked about him. Because I'm a preacher they told me about him. I hope you don't mind," said Reverend Jones.

"We don't mind. We're glad you're here," said Maggie.

They sat mostly silent for the next two hours when the nurse came back in. "The surgery is almost over. His vital signs are low, but he's still with us. Doctor Freeman will be out to talk to you when he's finished," she said.

Another family came in. Their son had been in a car accident. Reverend Jones went over and prayed with them while Maggie and Lucy sat with their hands folded in prayer for Avery.

Maggie thanked the nurse and poured herself another cup of coffee. She offered Reverend Jones a cup. He refused. He said coffee made him nervous. Lucy had fallen asleep. Maggie didn't wake her. She knew she must be exhausted.

Doctor Freeman came in looking like he had been through hell.

"Well, he made it through the surgery. He's not in good shape. I'm still not sure he'll survive," said Doctor Freeman.

Lucy stirred. "Is he alive? Is he alive?"

"Yes ma'am. He's alive. But, that's about all I can say. He'll be in critical care. You can go in one at a time. Try not to be emotional. He needs your positive support," said Doctor Freeman. "The nurse will let you know when you can go in."

"Thank you," said Maggie, sitting down beside Lucy, taking her hand.

The nurse called, "Mrs. Sutton, you can come in for a short time." Lucy looked at Maggie.

"I can't go with you. Only one can go," said Maggie. Lucy slowly followed the nurse down the hall to the curtained off area where nurses worked on their patients throughout the night. The R.N. was finishing up suctioning the fluid from Avery's lungs.

"Stop, you're hurting him," yelled Lucy.

"Ma'am, you have to remain calm or you can't stay," said the nurse.

"I don't want to see him like this. I can't take it," said Lucy, as she ran out of the ICU.

Maggie, saw her mother coming and ran to her helping her back to her chair. "He looks awful. He's going to die," cried Lucy.

"We don't know that. He's still alive and we have to concentrate on that," said Maggie, as she prepared herself to go in to see her daddy. But nothing she did prepared her for the way he looked. Avery had been pumped full of fluids. His eyeballs were outside his eyelids and he was swollen. He looked like a big frog lying there. There was a tube emerging from almost every part of his body and he lay still, unresponsive.

The ICU nurse came into the area. "He's on strong medications to keep him from waking up right away. Just speak softly to him. He can hear you," she said.

"Daddy, it's Maggie. You made it through the surgery. Things are going good. All you have to do now is heal. I love you. Mother and I are right outside your door." Maggie lowered her voice to a whisper, "Reverend Robby Jones is with us."

Maggie kissed her daddy on the cheek and left, wiping away tears as she went. She knew she had to encourage her mother as well as her daddy. "Mother, I think he's going to make it," she said.

At eight o'clock in the morning the nurse came to talk to the family again. "His vital signs have improved. He's not out of the woods yet, but things are looking up," she said. Reverend Jones went to the cafeteria, rejoicing, and brought back breakfast for everybody. You're going to be here for the long haul. You have to keep up your strength," he said.

Maggie thanked him. She was beginning to appreciate Reverend Jones more and more. As he left to go back to Boonetown, Maggie shook his hand and told him she appreciated him being with them and asked for his continued prayers.

Chapter 22

Stan had taken the pickup truck with temporary Alabama tags to Mobile. He wore ragged jeans and a work shirt. He checked into the Albert Pick Motel on Government Street around 10 a.m. under the name of Chester Moore. Chester Moore was a farmer from upstate Alabama. He was looking to talk to someone at the airport. He was thinking of taking flying lessons and becoming a crop duster. Their restaurant was still serving so he ate breakfast from the buffet. After breakfast Chester moseyed on over to the airport.

"Hello, anybody home?" Chester called. The attendant came out from the back room.

"Yes, sir, what can I do for you?" he asked.

"I'm Chester Moore. I don't know much about airplanes, but I figured you could tell me where I need to start in order to take flying lessons and learn how to crop-dust. Is that little red airplane out there a crop-duster?"

"No sir, that's a two-seater Cessna 182-B." Junior had identified the plane as a red, two-seater. The attendant continued, "Cessna makes a crop-duster, though. All of the crop-dusters are yellow so they can be seen easy because they fly so low to the ground."

"I've never seen an airplane like that before. Can I take a look at that one?" asked Chester.

"Sure, just don't fool with the controls. You need training before you can do that," laughed the attendant.

"Oh no, I won't bother nothing. I just want to set in the pilot's seat and see how it feels," said Chester.

"I guess it's alright. It can't hurt anything for you to look. When you finish looking, come back inside and I'll give you a pamphlet on where you can get flying lessons and where you may be able to buy a crop-duster, Cessna Ag-wagon," said the attendant.

Chester went to the plane. His aim was to get the N number. He found it and wrote it on his hand: 4756B Cessna. Now he would go to the registrar's office. But first he would get his crop-dusting information and tell the attendant how much he appreciated his help. The attendant would never know exactly how much he had helped.

The registrar's office was downtown Mobile. Chester walked in with his N number and asked to see the information on the plane. The lady at the desk said "I'm sorry, that plane is not registered to an individual. It is registered to a corporation and we're not allowed to give out that information. You'll have to go to the Federal Aviation Association in Washington D.C. to get that information." Chester's face grew grim and he cursed under his breath as he left the building. He would wait until he was on a secure phone to call his operative in Washington D. C. It was more complicated and a bigger operation than he had anticipated.

He wanted to get a look at the Mobile Port, so he went over there and began walking around. He noticed one shipment in particular— small crates labeled Butcher Agricultural Corporation. He approached one of the dock workers. "Where does all this stuff come from?" Chester asked, as if he were an inquisitive tourist.

Pointing to the small crates, "These come from Mexico," said the dock worker. "And these big ones come from some of the islands."

"What's in them?" asked Chester.

"Mostly agricultural products, but there's also shipments of coal and trinkets. It just depends, I guess, on what's been ordered," said the dock worker as he continued his work and ignored Chester.

The Farm

Upon arriving home Stan went to his office where he had a secure phone and called Mexico.

"Yes, Officer RDP78000-03 reporting in," said Stan.

"Yes sir, Agent 00781 here. What can I do for you, sir?"

"Check out an exporter, Butcher Agricultural Corporation, shipping to Port of Mobile Alabama in the United States from Mexico. I have reason to believe they are exporting heroin. Shut them down if you can."

"Yes, sir. We're on it," said the operative.

"Thank you. Keep in touch," said Stan, as he hung up and called Washington D.C.

"Officer RDP78-000-03 reporting in," said Stan.

"Yes sir, Agent 00960 here. How can I help sir?" said the agent.

"I need information on an aircraft. It's a Cessna 182-B Skylane, N number 4756B Cessna. I understand it's owned by a corporation. I want the name of the corporation and the name of the person that heads up the corporation. The Federal Aviation Association has that information and they are housed in various buildings around Washington, when you have what I need give me a call on my secure line."

"Yes, sir. I'll get on that right away," said the agent.

"I'll look forward to your call," said Stan, as he hung up the phone. He was tired and needed to eat something, but first he would try to call Maggie. Her phone rang and rang, but no one answered. *She must still be at the hospital with her daddy* thought Stan. *I'll just go over there after I freshen up a bit.* He went to the men's room and splashed water on his face. As he was leaving, he stopped by the snack room and got a Coke and a pack of peanuts. That would have to do. It was time to find Maggie.

Chapter 23

Maggie was in the cardio waiting room at the hospital. She and her mother had been there for almost four days. They were sitting quietly looking at magazines.

"Hello, beautiful," whispered Brian in Maggie's ear. Maggie jumped.

"Oh, you surprised me," she said. Lucy never looked up. She had become interested in a *True Story Romance* Magazine.

"How is he?" asked Brian.

"The good news is he's still alive. He has almost died more than once. He was having a heart attack when the ambulance brought him in. He hasn't awakened from the anesthesia yet, said Maggie. "The nurses have tried to bring him out a couple of times and he fights them, pulling out tubes. He'll have to be weaned off the hard stuff a little at a time."

"Have they let you see him?" asked Brian.

"We can go in to talk to him every three hours. They want us to be calm and positive," said Maggie. "He looks awful, but he's still with us."

"I know you're tired," said Brian.

"Yes, but I'm ok. How'd your trip go?"

"Things are looking up. I think we'll have what we're looking for by the first of next week," said Brian.

"I'm glad you're back," said Maggie.

"I am too. I'm wore out. I've only slept about four hours in the last three and a half days. I'm going home and sack out," said Brian. "I'll come by tomorrow."

"Good night, sleep tight," said Maggie, as Brian left.

Stan slept for ten hours. It was Sunday and Junior was home. Brian woke up to the smell of coffee and eggs.

As they began eating their eggs they talked. "What happened in Mobile?" asked Junior.

"I got a couple of leads and our operatives in Mexico and Washington D.C. are following up. We should have the information we need by tomorrow," said Stan.

"Speaking of Monday, isn't that the fifteenth? Have you got Maggie a birthday present yet?" asked Junior.

"No, I need to do that today. Do you have her something?" asked Stan.

"Yeah, I got her these patriotic socks with stars and stripes on them and some of those red-hot fire balls that she loves so much," said Junior. "You know she brought me socks for Christmas when we first met."

"I remember that," said Stan. "I have to think of something special. I'll go shopping this afternoon. Her daddy is still in the hospital. He's being kept asleep to help him heal. We should take a cake and ice cream to the hospital. We can take it in my cooler. Can you go tomorrow after you get out of school?"

"Say about six?" said Junior.

"Can you pick up some paper plates, plastic forks and napkins?" asked Stan. "I'll get the cake and ice cream when I go shopping for her present today."

"I can do that," said Junior. "What did you think of breakfast?"

"Thanks," said Stan. "Breakfast was good. It was nice to be home eating at my own table with a friend."

Stan went to the only jewelry store open on Sunday afternoon. He looked over their bracelets, but couldn't decide when his eyes landed on a silver necklace. It was a heart with the word 'LOOKOUT' written across it. He didn't know the intention of the designer, but he remembered his and Maggie's first kiss at the top of the big hill when he told her about 'Lookout point'. He asked the clerk to wrap the present for him and include a card that said, 'I remember'. Love Brian. He bought chocolate ice cream and chocolate cake, not because he thought Maggie liked it, but because he knew he and Junior liked it. He was still learning about what Maggie liked.

Brian and Junior arrived at the hospital about 6:15 p.m. and went straight to the cardio waiting room, but Maggie wasn't there. Lucy was sitting in the same chair she was in when Brian was there yesterday. He went over to her and asked, "Where's Maggie?"

"She's in visiting with her daddy," said Lucy.

"Are you Maggie's mother?" asked Brian.

"Yes, who're you?" asked Lucy.

"I'm a friend of Maggie's and Junior is with me. Do you know him?" asked Brian.

"I think I've seen him," said Lucy. "Why are you here?"

"We brought some cake and ice cream to celebrate Maggie's birthday," said Brian.

"It's Maggie's birthday?" asked Lucy.

"We'll surprise her when she gets back," said Brian. "And you can help us celebrate."

"I don't feel much like celebrating, but I'll try," said Lucy. "My husband is barely holding on."

Brian and Junior sat down to wait for Maggie. It was ten minutes before Brian saw her coming down the hall. "Get behind the door. Let's jump out and yell 'surprise'" said Brian.

"Surprise!" yelled the men. Lucy looked on, smiling.

"What? What're you doing?" asked Maggie.

"It's your birthday and we brought cake and ice cream," said Junior.

"How did you know it's my birthday? I don't recall telling either of you," said Maggie.

"Your daddy told Junior's daddy and Junior is a blabber mouth," said Brian, laughing.

"This is really nice," said Maggie, as they unpacked the goodies. Maggie cut Lucy a piece of cake and gave her a large spoonful of ice cream. "We really appreciate this. We've needed something to help us deal with the stress."

"I hope you like chocolate," said Brian.

"Who doesn't like chocolate?" said Maggie, not really saying she would have preferred vanilla. She loved her presents and when she opened the necklace, she gave Brian a knowing wink.

Brian and Junior stayed until visiting hours were over. "We're pulling for your daddy to get better," said Brian. He wanted to kiss Maggie goodbye, but didn't dare. He still wanted to keep their relationship a secret even from Junior. "I'll check on you tomorrow."

Brian went to bed wondering what J. Morris Higgins would be able to tell him about Reverend Jones. And, he had information for the prosecutor. They were finally getting somewhere.

The Farm

At 10:30 J. Morris walked into Stan's office. Stan was waiting. "Good morning, friend," J. Morris said, extending his hand.

"Good morning," said Stan. "Sit down, how've you been?"

"I'm doing well," said J. Morris. "How are you?"

"Better now that things are starting to shape up," said Stan. "I went to see Reverend Jones and found out he was released. What happened?"

"He has agreed to testify for the prosecution," said J. Morris.

"Wonderful. Who's his supplier?" asked Stan.

"He has named someone, but we're still investigating and I want to be very careful.

"Who is it?" asked Stan.

"This guy is high up and could easily slip through our fingers if he gets suspicious, he and the people who are helping him could flee the country," said J. Morris. "I want you to stay out of it so you have deniability," said J. Morris. "I don't want to blow your cover."

"That's hard for me. You know I want to know everything," said Stan.

"Yes, I know," said J. Morris. "What do you have for me?"

"A plane is dropping the heroin near Boonetown and likely other places. The drugs are coming in at the Port of Mobile, Alabama from B and A Corporation in Mexico. The plane belongs to the corporation and I think the head of the corporation is our very own John Butcher. I'm waiting on verified information I want you to subpoena John Butcher's phone records," said Stan.

"You know I can't do that without just cause. We'll have to arrest him first," said J. Morris.

"Do you have enough on him to make an arrest?" asked Stan. "I'll have more information by tomorrow."

"I believe we do. I'll take it to the grand jury. I want to do it by the book," said J. Morris.

"I agree. Keep me posted. I have some work to do here at The Farm and I have a friend I want to visit who's staying at the hospital with her daddy," said Stan.

"We'll talk again soon," said J. Morris, as he left Stan's office.

Stan's secure phone rang. "Officer RDP78-000-03 speaking."

"Agent 00960 here, sir. I have what you're looking for. The owner of the plane is the B and A Corporation or Butcher Agricultural Corporation operating out of Mexico and the head guy is John Butcher, a Kentucky senator living in Durant Kentucky."

"Bingo," said Stan. "Send me copies of the documents."

"Yes sir. They'll be in the mail tonight," said the agent.

Stan would let J. Morris know.

After seeing Maggie, Stan went back to his office and began preparing a witness list for J. Morris. Most of the people were locals but extradition papers would need to be filed on the pilot form Mobile. He should get the list to J. Morris soon. In the meantime, J. Morris had presented information to the Grand Jury. They would convene next week. He was hoping for an indictment. All of their proceedings would be done behind closed doors so there would be no possibility of the accused learning of the proceedings and escape the country.

Chapter 24

Maggie was excited when Brian came to the hospital to check on her. The hospital had just installed a television in the cardio waiting room and her daddy's vital signs had continued to improve. There were three other people waiting to see their loved ones and the news was playing on the TV. No one was paying much attention, but Brian stopped to watch: A huge drug ring had been shut down and arrests had been made in Juarez, Mexico. He secretly smiled.

The nurse came over to Maggie. "Your daddy has opened his eyes. I think you should go in and talk to him. He's scared. Reassure him. He's going to make it. He just needs to stay calm and heal," she said.

Maggie turned to Brian. "I need to go now. I'll probably stay twenty or thirty minutes with Daddy. If you can't come by tomorrow, I'll understand. We're doing fine."

"I'll try to run by. You know you can call me if you need anything," said Brian.

"I know," said Maggie, as she walked Brian to the elevator. She reached for his hand and gave it a loving squeeze.

Maggie went in the ICU to visit with her daddy. He was awake. His eyes were wild with fright. "Daddy, it's Maggie. You're doing fine. Don't be afraid," she said.

Avery was trying to talk, but he still had the respirator tube in his throat. "Don't try to talk. You'll be able to talk when they remove the respirator," said Maggie. "It won't be long. Just stay calm. I love you."

Avery's eyes relaxed and the tenseness went out of his body. Some of the tubes had been removed. He squeezed Maggie's hand. Lucy was standing outside the area wanting to come in so Maggie told her daddy she would see him next time she could visit and left.

"Mother, he's doing really good. Just let him know you love him," said Maggie.

"He knows I love him," said Lucy.

Avery continued to improve and by the end of the week he was completely off the respirator. The doctor said if he continued to do well, he would be able to go home in three more days. Lucy was frantic. "There's no way I can take him home and care for him. Besides that, I need to get back to work," she said.

"That's ok Mother," said Maggie. "I'm still out of school. I'll take him home with me."

"You'll have to," said Lucy. "I just can't deal with it."

So, in three days Maggie left the hospital and took her mother home to Boonetown. When she arrived back at the hospital her daddy had his papers signed and was ready to go to her house. The attending nurse told Maggie, "Make him do things for himself. You can either make an invalid out of him or help him get well."

Maggie understood and immediately encouraged him to walk to the car. The doctor told him he could resume normal activities such as sex as soon as he could walk around the block. He almost beat Maggie to the car. Maggie found that comical and thought her mother would be happy. Avery took the spare room and went straight to bed. Maggie proceeded to make dinner. Avery complained about how bad the food smelled and didn't want to eat. Maggie told him he had to eat something. This wasn't going to be easy.

For the next two weeks Maggie nursed her daddy back to health, encouraging him to eat and to get out of bed. He needed a shave. He cried and said he couldn't do it. Maggie told him he had to do it. He stood in front of the mirror in the bathroom and cried while shaving and Maggie stood in the kitchen and cried while making breakfast. It was hard being her daddy's parent, but she knew she had to be tough. When he asked if he could go home, Maggie knew he was better. He was missing Lucy and Lucy would take the following week off from work to be with him, so Maggie took Avery back to Boonetown.

Brian came over to see Maggie on Saturday after she took Avery home on Friday.

"I've missed you," he said.

"I've missed you, too," said Maggie. They were sitting on the couch watching a movie when during a commercial Brian changed the channel to see what else was on.

"We interrupt this program with breaking news," said the announcer. "John Butcher, a Kentucky state senator has been arrested on drug trafficking charges." They showed Senator Butcher being taken into custody by a police officer with a reporter running alongside them.

"Mr. Butcher, Mr. Butcher, what do you have to say about the charges?"

"This's all a mistake. I'm not guilty," said John Butcher, as they took him away to be fingerprinted and photographed.

Maggie and Brian sat in shock forgetting about their movie. "Did you know this was coming?" asked Maggie.

"I knew we were getting close. I didn't know when it would happen," said Brian. "J. Morris wants me to stay out of things from now on in. Nobody needs to know I've been helping with the investigation."

"I'm glad," said Maggie, snuggling up to Brian's shoulder. They sat for a while in silence. The movie no longer mattered. Just being together was enough. It was nearly twelve when Brian left. This time he made sure his good night kiss counted and Maggie kissed him back.

It was Monday before Brian called Maggie. "I just realized; we've never been on a date. Maggie, will you go on a date with me?"

"Well, I don't know. Where're you going to take me?" asked Maggie.

"How about I take you to that fancy restaurant across town where they have a band and dancing? Do you like dancing?" said Brian.

"I love dancing. My mother has always loved dancing. One of the first things I remember is mother dancing with me in her arms, but I've never had any formal dancing lessons. I might not dance the way you do," said Maggie.

"I've never had formal dancing lessons either. Most of the folks where I grew up square danced. We can make it up as we go," said Brian, laughing. "How does Friday night sound?"

"Friday night sounds great," said Maggie. "Say about seven?"

"Let's make it 6:00 so we can eat at the first setting," said Brian. "I think they have an early dinner and a late dinner. The band starts playing at 7:00."

"I'll see you on Friday," said Maggie. Maggie had not been on many dates. She and Tom had palled around at college and had gone to a few movies, but never dancing. In Boonetown there were very few boys in the neighborhood and none that Maggie wanted to date. She felt a little nervous. She had been asked out by a man she adored. She wondered how he really felt about her. Was she just a passing affair or could it develop into something more? A date, she thought. A real date.

The Farm

Stan had spent the past few days working at The Farm. His old friend and mentor who was the CEO at The Farm confided in him. "I'm turning seventy and I have a rare blood disease. I'm tired all the time. At the end of November, I'm going to retire and move to Florida."

He had always been there for Stan. Who would take his place? Stan couldn't imagine going to work and not having him around. And there was Junior. He would graduate soon and he had been recommended for the CIA Academy in Virginia to study to become an Officer. Stan would soon have the house to himself again. Jamie would come back to Durant the last day of August. He was sure of only one thing, change.

Jeff Newman began to hand off responsibilities to Stan, so Stan was busy from morning until night with little free time. Sometime in the next week the CEO would hand in his resignation and a request for applications would go out across the nation. Applications would be accepted for two months and a new man would be hired for the position. Stan was anxious. Not only was he losing his friend and mentor, he would be working for someone he may have never met, and there were still his undercover assignments—often dangerous and sometimes in a foreign country. Stan was sitting in his office thinking about his future when his phone rang. It was J. Morris. "Stan, I have something important to tell you. Can I come to your office now?"

"Yes," said Stan.

"Be prepared for a shocker," said J. Morris.

"It sounds intriguing," said Stan. "I'll see you in a bit."

Stan hurried to finish the report he was working on.

J. Morris walked into Stan's office. Stan jumped up from his seat. "What do you have to tell me?" he asked.

"Sit down. This is important. You need to stay calm. You're not going to believe this. I had a hard time digesting it myself. We have a match for the fingerprint in the glove found near Jenny's body," said J. Morris.

"A match. . . you mean we know who killed my wife? Who is the bastard? I'll tear him apart with my bare hands," said Stan, standing up and banging his right fist into his left palm.

"Sit down," said J. Morris. "You're going to have to control yourself. We still have to prove this in court."

"I know. I understand I still have to remain aloof. Who is it?"

"Our forensic expert matched the print in the glove to the print we took from John Butcher last weekend," said J. Morris. "Now I need a witness list for Jenny's murder trial. It looks like we can tie the drug trafficking and the murder together. John Butcher is being questioned and charged with Jenny's murder as we speak."

"This has taken so long, and yet it's a shock," said Stan, as he began to sob.

J. Morris went over and put his arm around Stan. "I know this has been hard on you. You've been a rock," said J. Morris.

"I'm sorry for the tears. It's the first time I've cried. Up until now I've been able to distance myself and look at the evidence as just another case, but today it has hit home. He murdered my wife. He murdered my little girl's mother. He's a God damned murderer and I hope he rots in prison," said Stan.

"We'll do our best to make that happen," said J. Morris. "Can I get you something?"

"Got any Kentucky Bourbon?" asked Stan.

"We can get a beer at the bar on West Street. Let's go. It'll do you good to get out of the office for a while. I'm buying," said J. Morris. It took about ten minutes to walk to the bar. The fresh air felt good. While there, they had a hamburger and fries. Stan ate only a few bites, but the company was just what he needed.

When Stan returned to his office, he sat at his desk looking at the triangle designs in the wallpaper on the wall, thinking about Jenny, wondering how he could have let this happen. *And, I'm about to go on a date? My wife has been murdered and I'm dating already? No, I can't do this. I have to cancel my date with Maggie.*

He picked up the phone and held it in his hand. He had to make the call. "Hello, Maggie. This is Brian."

"Good afternoon. How are you?" came the carefree voice of Maggie.

"Maggie, I'm sorry," started Brian.

"Sorry? Sorry for what?" said Maggie.

"Maggie, I know I asked you to go dancing with me tonight, but I can't," said Brian.

"Can't? What's wrong?" asked Maggie.

"I'm not feeling well. I gave J. Morris your phone number. He's supposed to call to see if you can go with him tomorrow to talk to your daddy. If it's alright I'll come over on Sunday afternoon and explain what's happening. I'm just not in any shape to have a fun night out right now. I hope you can understand," said Brian.

"I was really looking forward to our night out. I'll try to understand. You say J. Morris will call me today?" said Maggie. "I was going for a run, but I'll stay near the phone so I don't miss his call. I know he needs to get things lined up for the trial. It's in a week and a half, right?

"Yes, the trial is coming up soon. I suspect he'll call sometime within the next hour. He's usually pretty prompt," said Brian.

"Please forgive me. You don't deserve to be treated this way. We'll talk on Sunday," said Brian.

"We'll talk," said Maggie.

Chapter 25

John Butcher was taken to the county jail for questioning, but he refused to answer any questions without his lawyer present. He called. His lawyer was out of town. After all it was the weekend. It would be Monday before he could get into contact with him. He would just have to relax and spend the weekend with the riffraff. Jake Milton, Esquire was well into his sixties and known throughout Kentucky. He was often called on in high-profile cases. He and his wife were spending time at their summer island home. John Butcher felt sure he would soon be free of the charges. Jake Milton had been his friend for more than thirty years. He had gotten him out of scrapes before and he was certain he would do it again.

On Monday Jake Milton came to the jail. "What have you done now?" he asked, half laughing.

"They can't prove anything. They say I'm heading up a drug trafficking ring. They've arrested some people at my plant in Mexico, but they can't prove I had anything to do with it," said Butcher.

"We'll get you a bail hearing set and go from there," said his lawyer.

"How long is that going to take? These roughens hang around like they're going to attack and I noticed one of them has a knife," said John Butcher.

"Relax, we'll have you out of here in no time," said Jake Milton.

The bail hearing was set for Tuesday at 2.00 p.m. J. Morris went to argue the case:

"Your honor, John Butcher is a prominent citizen with money. He has access to an airplane and business associates in Mexico. He is a definite flight risk. I recommend bail be denied."

Jake Milton came prepared: "Your honor, John Butcher is a prominent citizen. That's exactly the reason he will not leave the country. He will defend his honor in court. His constituents believe in him and he will not let them down."

Judge Parker was a hard man to deal with. He did not grant bail lightly. "I will take these arguments into consideration. We are adjourned until 3:30 today when I will give you my decision."

"I thought you said I would be out of here," said John Butcher. "I pay you enough. You should do your job."

"We just happened to draw Judge Parker. If it hadn't happened on the weekend, I could have made a few contacts and arranged for a better judge. Right now, we just have to take what we've got. I didn't have enough time," said Jake Milton.

The police officer came and took John Butcher in handcuffs back to his cell to wait until the judge was ready. John Butcher was fuming mad. *How could this happen? Just wait until I'm out and back in charge. I'll get Judge Parker relieved of his job. I have influence. I'm somebody to be dealt with. I'll show them.* He folded his hands and sat down on his cot to wait.

Although it was only an hour and a half, it seemed like hours before the jailer came to take John Butcher back to the courtroom. J. Morris was already seated in the prosecutor's chair. Jake Milton came in just as John Butcher arrived.

"All rise," said the bailiff. The judge came in looking concerned. "Be seated," he said.

"I'm distraught. I had almost come to the conclusion to grant bail when my assistant came in and told me someone is trying to influence my decision. Ladies and gentlemen, I am here to tell you I cannot be bought. Your efforts are in vain. Bail is hereby denied. Trial is set for August first beginning at eight o'clock in the morning." John Butcher looked at Jake Milton as he sat stunned with his mouth open. "Did you try to buy him off?" asked Butcher.

"Not exactly," said Jake Milton. "I'm sorry. You'll just have to grin and bear it for a couple of weeks. That'll give me a chance to build your case."

Chapter 26

Maggie felt like the breath had been knocked out of her. What was going on? Had Brian decided he didn't want to date her after all? Had he changed his mind? Was there someone else? Had she been reading too much into his attention and his kisses? Was he just playing with her? What would Sunday bring? The phone brought her back to reality. "Hello, Maggie speaking."

"Ms. Adams, this is J. Morris Higgins. I'm the lawyer prosecuting the case against John Butcher. Did Brian tell you I would call?"

"Yes, he told me," said Maggie.

"He said you would probably agree to go with me to take a statement from your father. He put him on the witness list, but I understand he's recovering from heart surgery and should not be asked to testify in court?" said J. Morris.

"That's right, he's not exactly on his feet yet and stress is very bad for his heart condition," said Maggie.

"We'll try our best not to upset him," said J. Morris.

"I could tell you what he told me if that would help," said Maggie.

"That's hearsay and not admissible in court. It's best if I get his statement," said J. Morris. "Will you be available to go to Boonetown at 10 tomorrow?"

"Yes, that'll be fine," said Maggie. "Do you have my address?"

"Yes, Brian gave it to me. I'll pick you up at 10," said J. Morris.

"I'm not going to tell daddy we're coming. He would worry and fret all night. We'll just show up and take it from there," said Maggie. He's going to be leery of anyone who is associated with the arrest of one of his friends."

"That's probably a wise idea. I'll see you tomorrow," said J. Morris.

Maggie hung up the phone and immediately began worrying about how the encounter would affect her daddy. He was still fragile. And she had promised she wouldn't tell anyone about him finding the dope. Would she have to tell her daddy she had betrayed his confidence? How would her mother react? Maybe she could distract her mother. She didn't have to know. She would call her mother and tell her she was coming for a visit tomorrow, that way her mother could go to her sister's house for a while. She would be there between eleven and twelve to stay with her daddy. She told her not to tell her daddy. She wanted to surprise him. Maybe Lucy would take the bait. She was always looking for a way to get out of the house and she hadn't seen her sister in over a month.

That night it was Maggie who stayed awake, tossing and turning all night. She was glad when morning came. She was up early, dressed and out the door for a run. She came back around 9, took a shower, changed clothes and ate a bowl of cereal. If J. Morris was as prompt as Brian said he was, he would be there soon. She went to the front porch to wait. Birds were flitting here and there. A hummingbird was at the feeder. She poured some fresh nectar into the feeder jar. The morning air was cool and refreshing. J. Morris pulled in the driveway just as she sat down.

"Good morning," said J. Morris. "I see you're ready to go?"

"Yes, I'm ready. I know this is necessary, but I'm really nervous about upsetting Daddy," said Maggie.

"I'll try my best to keep him calm," said J. Morris. On the way to Boonetown Maggie and J. Morris made small talk. J. Morris told Maggie about how he and Brian had been in school together and how they had been friends for years. How they had married about the same time and how his wife was an attorney and how they both had little girls. "How do you know Brian?" he asked.

"I was his daughter's teacher last year when his wife went missing. His little girl was able to talk to me and we bonded. She's precious," said Maggie. "After this trial is over, I hope she'll be able to come back to live in Durant. It's been hard on her to live apart from her daddy."

"This whole affair has been rough on everyone," said J. Morris. "I'll be glad when we have it over and done with."

"Turn at the next road," said Maggie. "My daddy's farm is a little far out in the country, right near the Jungle. Have you heard of the Jungle?"

"You know, I did read about it once. It was a virgin forest until the 1930s when the depression hit. I understand they cut many of the huge trees and sold the lumber. It's a pity. I guess they needed the money," said J. Morris.

"Time changes everything and money makes the world go round," said Maggie. "The Jungle's still a wild and wooly place. My daddy and his buddies go hunting in there. Did Brian tell you Daddy has the Kentucky coonhound champion? His name is Banjo. He won the time trials this last May. That might be a place where you could start a conversation with Daddy. He's awful proud of that dog."

"It does help if I know a little something about your daddy. He sounds like an interesting fellow," said J. Morris.

"What can I say? He's my daddy," said Maggie. "I want to protect him."

"Of course, you do. That's natural. But if possible, let him answer my questions. It might even work better if you go out of the room. I promise I won't badger him. I'll be gentle," said J. Morris.

"I'll try my best to stay out of the questioning," said Maggie. "I know I would have a tendency to want to help him."

"I'm glad you understand," said J. Morris, as they pulled into the yard at the Sutton farm.

Lucy was coming out the front door. "I'm going over to Polly's. I'll be back in about an hour," said Lucy.

"I understand," said Maggie. "You go and enjoy your visit. We'll stay until you get back."

"Who's the good-looking guy?" asked Lucy, in Maggie's ear.

"Don't be reading anything into this. He's just a friend who agreed to come with me today. He had never been to Boonetown and he had heard about daddy's coonhound. We'll be here when you get back. Have a good time," said Maggie.

Maggie and J. Morris went into the living room where Avery was stretched out in a lounge chair. "Daddy, this is my friend J. Morris Higgins," said Maggie. "We have some news to tell you and J. Morris has a few questions he needs to ask you."

Avery sat up and shook J. Morris's hand. "What kind of questions? I don't like answering questions. I don't think I'll know the answers," said Avery. "What's the news?"

"I don't know if you've watched TV lately? You might have seen it on the news. John Butcher, the man from Durant who has been coming to go hunting with you was arrested for drug trafficking," said Maggie.

"No, not John Butcher. There must be some kind of mistake. He seems like a nice fellow," said Avery.

"Nothing has been proven in court," said Maggie. "You may be right. I hope you are."

"I just don't know what to think anymore," said Avery.

J. Morris is talking to people who know Senator Butcher and needs to ask you some questions. Do you think you can answer a few for him?" asked Maggie

"What does he think I'll know?" asked Avery.

"You may not know anything. There're no right or wrong answers to my questions, all I need is for you to tell me what you remember," said J. Morris. "I've written down some questions and I'll pencil in your answers and have you sign that what I have written is correct. Maggie can witness that you signed and I'll put my notary seal on it. We'll present this paper to the judge and your presence in court will not be required."

"If I answer your questions I won't have to go to court?"

"That's right. I'll take the signed paper and you will not have to go," said J. Morris.

"I'll try," said Avery.

Maggie moved over to the other side of the room and began looking out the window.

"State your name for the court," said J. Morris.

"You want me to say my name?" asked Avery.

"Yes sir, just say your name," said J. Morris.

"Avery Sutton?"

"Yes sir, thank you. Do you know a man by the name of John Butcher?"

"Yes."

"When did you first become acquainted with Senator Butcher?"

"I didn't know he was a senator. He and this songwriter fellow came up here about a year ago and said they were coon hunters and had heard about my dogs. They wanted to come and take their dogs out with mine to train them better," said Avery.

"And did they come?"

"Yeah, they came almost every Friday night. Their dogs weren't much good and they definitely needed training."

"Where did you take them hunting?"

"We went to the Jungle. There's a lot of animals in there and I keep the animals hides and sell the fur. It pays for groceries," said Avery, smiling.

"Did you ever see anything unusual out of John Butcher?"

"One night he and that songwriter fellow left the group early. And he seemed to know Robby Jones, the Pentecostal pastor. They would get off to the side and talk some," said Avery. "I didn't think too much about it."

"Is there anything else you can tell me?"

"Well, I don't know if I should tell you and I'll probably be in trouble, but I saw an airplane dump out something up around the Jungle. I went back there to see what they dumped and it was a box of drugs. I reckon it was drugs. I don't have much experience with dope, myself," said Avery.

"Do you know what kind of airplane it was that dumped the drugs?" asked J. Morris.

"One of them little ones," said Avery.

J. Morris read the statements back to Avery. Have I written down everything correctly?" he asked.

"Yeah, that's what I said alright," said Avery.

"Then if it's correct, sign here on this line," said J. Morris, pointing to the signature line. Avery's hand was a little shaky, but he managed to sign.

"Maggie, I need you to sign as a witness," said J. Morris. Maggie came over and signed on the witness line.

"Well, I think that's got it. Thank you, Mr. Sutton. You did a good job. Maggie and I said we would stay until your wife gets home. Now where's that champion coonhound I've heard so much about?" said J. Morris.

"He's out in the backyard. Come on I'll show you. Did you see my trophy?" Avery walked over to the mantel and pulled the trophy off and handed it to J. Morris.

J. Morris held it up and took a good look. "This is really special," said J. Morris, as they went to the backyard to get acquainted with Banjo.

Maggie sat by the window and was thankful for J. Morris. He had managed to get her daddy to tell him about the plane dumping the dope without her having to admit she had told. Her daddy seemed to be doing better. His mind was clearer.

Lucy came running in about ten after twelve. "I was afraid you'd be gone," she said.

"I told you we'd stay until you got back. How was Aunt Polly?" asked Maggie.

"Oh, she's alright, always complaining about something. Her hairdresser put too much cream rinse on her hair and she thinks it has made her hair greasy. Her hair didn't look greasy to me and I told her so, but she didn't think much of my opinion," said Lucy.

"Daddy and J. Morris are out playing with Banjo. I'll go get them. We'll need to head back," said Maggie. "I'll stay longer next time so we can talk. Daddy looks like he's doing well."

"Yeah, I'll go back to work Monday. He can stay by himself now. The other day he looked at me and said, 'I'm home' ain't I?" said Lucy. "I think that was the first time he knew where he was. I don't think he remembers being at your house."

"It does take a while to get to thinking right after heart surgery. He had a rough time. I'm so thankful he's going to be alright," said Maggie, as she went to the back door to let J. Morris know Lucy was home.

On the way back to Durant J. Morris told Maggie he really enjoyed meeting her daddy. Maggie felt good about the interview and hoped it would be valuable in the trial. John Butcher had used her daddy for his own purposes and was probably responsible for Junior being on drugs. Things like that were not supposed to happen in a cozy little town tucked away in the hills of Kentucky. She had always felt safe and protected there, but Boonetown was changing.

J. Morris said he would be working around the clock until the trial. He was still fearful John Butcher would slip through his fingers, but his case was beginning to come together and he was becoming more confident each day. The witness list Brian provided had proven to be valuable.

Maggie was quiet. The mention of Brian brought back his phone call from yesterday. She had no idea what to expect on Sunday afternoon. Her heart ached and she heaved a sigh. Waiting was not one of her strong suits. It was two o'clock when J. Morris dropped her off at her house. She made herself a peanut butter sandwich and drank a Coke for lunch. She felt depleted. Her body was tired. Sleep had escaped her the night before. She turned on the TV and lay down on the couch and soon fell into a deep sleep.

She slept hard. The next thing she knew it was six o'clock and the news was on: "Senator John Butcher has been charged with the murder of a young woman from Pilot Ridge, Kentucky. She has been missing since November of last year. Last week her body was discovered in Salt Creek by hunters near her childhood home. Senator Butcher was earlier charged with drug trafficking. His trial begins next week. Maggie sat up wide awake. *That's Jenny*, she thought. *I wonder if Brian knows. I'm sure J. Morris knew today while we were at Boonetown. He didn't mention it. No, he wouldn't discuss things like that with an outsider like me before the trial. What else was going to happen?* Her mind was going crazy. She wondered just what else John Butcher was mixed up in. She never liked his looks. She had seen his picture in the newspaper once. He looked shifty and she couldn't understand why her daddy had trusted him. Her daddy hadn't seemed to be bothered too much by the news. It was because of the way J. Morris had handled the situation. He put her daddy at ease and he appeared authentic. He was an easy person to trust.

The phone rang. It was Brian. "Maggie, good you're home, how did it go with J. Morris and your dad?"

"It went ok. J. Morris put Daddy at ease and Daddy even told him about the airplane and the drugs," said Maggie.

"I thought he would do a good job," said Brian. "I've been thinking. I don't want to wait until tomorrow. Can I come over now? I really do need to talk to you," said Brian.

"Now? Well ok," said Maggie.

"I'll be there in about fifteen minutes," said Brian.

Maggie washed her face, brushed her hair and freshened her make-up. She was anxious. The doorbell rang. It was Brian.

"Come in," said Maggie. The two of them went in and sat down in the living room. Brian sat on the couch and Maggie sat down in the big chair across from him. Brian gazed at the floor. The silence was stifling. Brian looked at Maggie. "We have a match for the fingerprint in the glove found near Jenny's body," he said.

"I heard—. . ." said Maggie. Brian interrupted. "The print belongs to John Butcher. The sonofabitch killed my Jenny." He began to sob.

Maggie went over and sat down by Brian. She wanted to put her arms around him, but didn't know if she should. She touched his shoulder.

"It has hit me like a ton of bricks. My stomach is in knots and all I can do is cry. That's the reason I had to break our date. My wife is dead and John Butcher killed her. My beautiful Jenny is dead, gone forever and I'll never get her back," said Brian.

Brian and Maggie sat for a while without talking. Then Brian stood up and walked toward the front door. "I need some time," he said.

"It's ok. I understand," said Maggie, as Brian left, but she wasn't sure she did understand and she definitely wasn't ok. Was he breaking up with her?

Chapter 27

Maggie had a busy week with in-service training for the new school year. Her new class would be energetic and exciting. She was working hard on making sure she had read each child's folder and placement records. This year she had more boys than girls, so her activities would reflect a great deal of movement. Maggie wondered if Jamie would come to school as Mary Alice or Jamie? She pondered how her favorite little girl would handle third grade? She would be a year younger than most of the children in her class and yet she was so far ahead academically. She wondered how often she would be able to see Jamie? Maggie felt she and Brian had left their relationship hanging. She had no idea where she stood. Obviously, they had rushed into something before Brian was ready and she understood he needed time, but how much time? Would they ever be together again?

Junior would graduate from Narcotics School on Friday. Maggie risked a phone call. Brian answered. "This is Maggie. Is Junior there?" asked Maggie.

"Yes," said Brian. "I'll get him."

Just hearing Brian's voice made Maggie's heart beat faster and she caught her breath in a sigh as Junior answered the phone.

"Hello," said Junior.

"Hey cousin, I hear you're graduating on Friday. Do you have plans for Friday night?"

"No, I haven't made any plans," said Junior.

"How about I fix you a graduation celebration dinner?" said Maggie.

"That sounds like fun," said Junior.

"What would you like?" asked Maggie.

"Maybe fried chicken, potato salad and green beans?" said Junior.

"And chocolate cake and ice cream?" asked Maggie.

"I'm hungry already," said Junior. "I'll be there on Friday about 6 o'clock."

"See you than," said Maggie, as she hung up the phone.

After his graduation on Friday, Junior packed up the old truck and headed over to Maggie's house. He helped put dinner on the table. Maggie said frying chicken wasn't her best suit, but Junior said everything was delicious.

"I can't believe we're cousins," said Junior. "Brian thought we might be dating. He asked me about it."

"I think Brian is having a really difficult time," said Maggie.

"I can't imagine losing a wife like he did," said Junior. "He told me it would be better for me and my career if I never marry."

"I just know he's hurting," said Maggie.

"He told me how much he appreciates all that you're doing for his little girl," said Junior.

They made small talk until about eight o'clock and Junior said he had better head to Boonetown before his parents went to bed and locked him out. Maggie kissed him on the cheek and sent him packing. "Don't let anything stand in your way," she said. "You'll be the best narcotics officer ever."

"Thanks for believing in me," said Junior, as he got in the truck and drove away.

Maggie went back into the house and sat down to think. *Yes, Brian appreciates me and that's all it is. He's grateful for all I've done for Jamie. I'll never be anymore to him than Jamie's teacher.*

Chapter 28

Stan realized he had made the decision to bring Jamie back to Durant when Junior asked him about going to Maggie's house for his celebration dinner. He told Junior he had to go to Missouri to get Jamie. He couldn't tell Junior about what was happening with him and Maggie. It was best unsaid.

He left on Friday morning to spend the night with his parents and bring Jamie back to Durant. He found comfort in talking with his dad who had figured out years ago Stan was working for the CIA. He'd been an intelligence officer in World War II and understood the force that was driving Stan.

"I think we're about to bring the investigation to a close. The trial begins on Monday. John Butcher has been arrested for Jenny's murder and for drug trafficking," said Stan.

"I saw it on the news. I know you'll do what you have to do," said his dad.

"The prosecutor wants me to stay out of it, if possible," said Stan.

"That's a good idea, especially with Jamie coming back to be with you," said his dad.

"My old friend and mentor's leaving his post at The Farm," said Stan. "Just between you and me, I'm mulling over the idea of applying for his job. It's been rough on Jamie with me out of town so much and taking on dangerous assignments."

"But, will you be satisfied being a family man?" asked his dad.

"That's what I'm trying to figure out," said Stan.

On the way back to Durant, Jamie began to ask questions: "Will I be Jamie Turner or Mary Alice Scott this year? Why didn't Ms. Maggie come with you? Will my mommy be gone forever? What's third grade like? Are my friends still at my old school? Can we go on a picnic again sometime? Will you have to go away and leave me with grandpa and grandma again?"

"You're just full of questions," teased Stan, but deep inside he wished he knew the answers. He had as many questions as Jamie and he was the only one who could answer them. He just wasn't ready to deal with confronting the questions that plagued his thoughts. Maybe having Jamie home would give him more insight into his future.

The next day he took Jamie to school and talked with her new teacher. She remained Mary Alice Scott. Her teacher remembered her from the year before and was impressed with her test scores. "Because she is younger than the other children, we'll need to pay special attention to her social development, said her teacher. "It would be good if she had a special friend that's her age."

"I'll work on it," said Stan, as he left for work.

He was busy. The day appeared to fly by and it was time to pick Jamie up. She was waiting with her classmates and her teacher. He saw Maggie with her class. He sighed as he opened the door for Jamie. She climbed in the front seat.

"How was your day?" Stan asked.

"I like my teacher, I guess. But I really miss Ms. Maggie," she said. "Can we go over to her house? I really didn't get to talk to her today. She was too busy and I couldn't leave my class to go see her. Please?"

"It was the first day of school for Ms. Maggie, too. She'll be tired today. Let's wait and I'll call her and we'll arrange a time to go see her," said Stan.

"Can we go on another picnic? I love picnics," said Jamie.

"We'll see," said Stan. "Do you want a grilled cheese for dinner?"

"That'll be alright. I'd rather have one of Ms. Maggie's hamburgers," said Jamie.

"When I go to the store, I'll buy some hamburger meat and buns so we can have hamburgers tomorrow night," said Stan.

"You're the best daddy ever," said Jamie, giving Stan a hug. That was just what he needed. He was glad Jamie was home.

Chapter 29

John Butcher was impatient and angry. The past two weeks he had been required to clean his room, including the toilet. Once he had kitchen duty and was on the schedule to do laundry. He threw his shoe against the wall. *I'm being treated unfairly. This is beneath my dignity. No man of my statue should be treated this way.* Jake Milton visited often and talked about their case. He wanted John Butcher to ask for a plea deal, but John Butcher insisted he wanted to stand up for his rights. He even wanted to testify on his own behalf. Jake Milton hoped he would change his mind, but there was a determination. John Butcher knew what he was doing. He was in charge.

Stan was on the way to The Farm, but instead drove straight to the courthouse where the trial was in progress. He slipped into a seat on the back row.

The judge was sitting erect and serious. "John Butcher, please stand," he said.

John Butcher stood. Jake Milton stood with him.

"Mr. Butcher, the state has charged you with two counts: Count number one, the murder of Virginia Anderson. Sir, how do you plead?" asked the judge.

"Not guilty," said John Butcher, shifting from his right foot to his left.

"Count number two-drug trafficking for the purpose of resell. How do you plead?" said Judge Parker.

"Not guilty," said John Butcher.

"Let the record show the defendant has pled not guilty on both counts," said Judge Parker. "We'll adjourn until one o'clock when we'll begin jury selection."

Stan had his first up-close look at John Butcher. Until now he had only seen pictures. John Butcher was round and chubby, about five feet, five inches tall, slightly bald, a mousy little man without a face.

Feeling sick to his stomach and angry, Stan left before J. Morris saw him.

Jury selection began on time. Judge Parker questioned the entire group. Do any of you know John Butcher personally? Do any of you have prior knowledge about this trial? Are any of you acquainted with either of the lawyers? If so, please excuse yourselves now. Three of the fifty people gathered left the room. The first twelve people were brought into the courtroom. The lawyers would have their turn at questions. District Attorney, J. Morris Higgins wanted as many women on the jury as possible. He felt they would lean more in his direction. On the other hand, Jake Milton was vying for men. He believed they would understand John Butcher's point of view. The lawyers questioned thirty-two people. When all was said and done, there were five women and seven men on the jury. The two alternates were women.

"We'll begin with opening remarks tomorrow morning at eight o'clock," said Judge Parker. "Court is adjourned."

When morning came the courthouse was alive with activity. The jury had taken their seats, the lawyers were in their chairs and the defendant was brought to the court shackled in handcuffs. The stenographer sat erect ready to take down every word for the record.

"All rise," said the bailiff. The judge appeared stern faced and took his place.

"You may be seated," said the bailiff.

"We're here today to begin the proceedings against John Butcher with the first count being the murder of Virginia Anderson and the second count of drug trafficking for the purpose of resell. Mr. Butcher, do you understand the allegations brought against you?" asked Judge Parker.

John Butcher rose to his feet. "Yes, your honor," he said.

"Then, we'll proceed with opening remarks, Counselor, are you ready?" the judge asked, looking at J. Morris.

"Yes, your honor." He stood and walked to the middle of the room, addressing the jury:

"The defense will have you believe John Butcher is an honorable man and he could not possibly have committed these heinous crimes, but the prosecution will prove without a doubt John Butcher is not an honorable man and he has indeed committed these crimes. Virginia Anderson, a young woman who worked at the State Department alongside John Butcher was brutally murdered and her body disposed of in Salt Creek up in the mountains where her assailant thought no one would ever discover it. Hunters found her body and as a result evidence has been secured pointing directly at John Butcher. We'll show you how John Butcher has appeared to the public as a noble, caring individual while in his private life and through back channels is an entirely different person. There is a different side to John Butcher and we intend to bring his underside to light.

J. Morris pulled his jacket off and laid it on his chair. He wanted to appear casual and personal to the jury. "John Butcher is not only a murderer, but he is responsible for thousands of ruined lives. He's responsible for most of the heroin that's being peddled to your children and your grandchildren." J. Morris had noticed two of the men and one woman was likely in their sixties and no doubt could have grandchildren.

"The prosecution will show you without a doubt how John Butcher brought drugs into our peaceful little towns throughout southern Kentucky. John Butcher is not the honorable senator he pretends to be. He may have won the election, but he has not shown his true colors. We'll show you who he really is. We'll present evidence to show he's responsible for these crimes. But it's you who has the ability to prevent him from continuing his misdeeds. You and you alone have the ability to bring John Butcher to justice. Thank you for your attention."

The jury was awake and listening. J. Morris thought he had reached them with his comments. But now it was Jake Milton's turn. He rose with his thumbs in his belt and sauntered to the middle of the aisle.

"Well, that was an impressive display of hogwash," he said. "My client is indeed a respectable man, elected three times to the Kentucky legislature. Millions of people adore him. He reaches out to people and helps his constituents wherever he's needed. He's a compassionate man with a reputation bar none. We'll show you a man of valor, a man who could not possibly have committed these crimes. Senator Butcher was nowhere near Virginia Anderson when she died. He has had neither access nor motive.

While he has acquisitions in other countries, he's not always directly involved in the day-to-day operations. A man of his stature and varied interests may not be aware of all that happens within a company he owns. I understand some of his employees have been arrested in Mexico. His employees were arrested. Does that mean he's guilty? I think not. My client is not guilty of the charges brought against him and the evidence will prove he's not guilty. If the evidence doesn't fit, you must acquit. Thank you

"Thank you, gentlemen. We'll break for lunch. Be back at two o'clock when the prosecution will begin your case, said the judge, looking at J. Morris.

"All rise," said the bailiff.

Everyone filed out of the courtroom. John Butcher was taken back to his cell. Jake Milton brought him a dinner from a local restaurant.

"There's enough here for a king," said John Butcher. "You must think this is my last meal."

"I just want you to look fat and healthy for what's coming next," said Jake Milton.

The Farm

Stan went to Jeff Newman's office. Jeff was going through his desk and files, throwing away things no longer needed. He looked tired.

"How's the search for a new chief going?" asked Stan.

"We have twenty applications. The Board will decide in a couple of weeks. I'm glad I'm not in charge of that. I know several of the guys and it would be hard to choose," said Jeff.

"I've been thinking about applying for the job," said Stan.

"Really? I thought you were satisfied with your job. You'll be the top guy in a couple of years. I never thought of you settling down in a small town. What's going on?" asked Jeff.

"This thing with Jenny has made me take a hard look at my life. I have a lot of regrets. If I had been more attentive and out of town less, Jenny might still be alive. I have a daughter to raise. I have to protect her," said Stan.

"What has happened with her teacher?" asked Jeff.

"She has a different teacher this year," said Stan.

"What are you not telling me?" said Jeff.

"You know me too well. I asked her for a date, but broke it after John Butcher was arrested." said Stan.

"Give it time. You'll figure it out. You need time to grieve," said Jeff.

"That may be another reason I don't need to be on the road," said Stan.

"About that. You're sure you want to apply for this job?"

"Yes, I'm through running around the world chasing criminals," said Stan.

Jeff reached in the file cabinet and pulled out an application packet. "Fill this out and return it to me today, if possible. I'll be glad to write you a letter of recommendation," said Jeff.

"This'll take all day. What do they want to know?" asked Stan.

"You know, just about everything," said Jeff, laughing.

"I'd better go get started," said Stan.

"Wait, have you heard from Junior? How's he doing?"

"He called and gave me his contact information. He's settled in and working hard," said Stan.

"Glad to hear it. He's a fine young man," said Jeff.

"I'll bring this back this afternoon," said Stan, as he left.

Chapter 30

At one o'clock the courtroom was beginning to fill with witnesses and curious on lookers. Stan had managed to sneak away from work to catch a few minutes of the trial before going to pick up Jamie. He stayed out of sight, not wanting J. Morris to know he was there.

"All rise," came the solemn demand from the bailiff.

Judge Parker entered dressed in his black robe looking refreshed and ready, motioning toward J. Morris. "Call your first witness."

"The State calls Marie Butcher to the stand," said J. Morris.

John Butcher turned in surprise toward the witness.

"Raise your right hand. Do you swear to tell the truth, the whole truth and nothing but the truth?" asked the bailiff.

"I, I do," she said. Her hands were shaking. She was of average height, slim and blond. Her white pencil skirt and light blue blouse gave her an air of sophistication.

"State your name for the court," said Judge Parker.

"My name is Marie Butcher," she said.

J. Morris approached the stand, about three feet away. "How do you know the defendant?" he asked.

"He was my husband," she said.

"He was your husband? Does that mean you're now divorced?"

"Yes," she said.

"Did you have a good marriage?" asked J. Morris.

"Objection," yelled Jake Milton. "What does her marriage to my client have to do with this case?"

"It speaks to John Butcher's character," said J. Morris.

"I'll allow it," said the judge. "Answer the question."

"No, our marriage was tumultuous and short. We were married only five years," said Marie Butcher.

"Why did you divorce?" asked J. Morris.

"He was not the man I thought I married. He became emotional, angry and abusive. I couldn't live with him any longer," she said.

"Thank you," said J. Morris, looking toward Jake Milton. "Your witness."

"Mrs. Butcher, did you love your husband?" asked Jake Milton.

"Well, yes. I supposed I did at first," she said.

"Isn't it true you were the one who was angry and emotional? Did you not frequently hand out verbal abuse? Did you not agitate and goad your husband into anger?" asked Jake Milton.

"I may have. I may have called him names sometimes," she said.

"Names? Didn't you call him the worst kind of names? Didn't you try to make him angry?" asked Jake Milton. "Any man would be hurt and angry. Senator Butcher is no different. He's just human.

"Thank you, that's all for now," said the defense lawyer.

"Redirect?" asked the judge.

"Yes, Mrs. Butcher, what name did you call Senator Butcher?" asked J. Morris.

"I called him 'little man'," she said.

"What did John Butcher do when you called him, 'little man'?"

"The last time I did it he grabbed me by the throat and choked me until I almost passed out. I managed to get away. That's when I left him and filed for divorce," she said.

"And why did you call him 'little man'?

Marie Butcher turned red in the face and cast her eyes down. "Because he had a hard time performing sexually," she said.

"Thank you, no further questions," said J. Morris.

"Call your next witness," said the judge.

"The state calls Julie Stern," said J. Morris. Julie was sworn in and J. Morris began questioning her. "What is your profession?" he asked.

"I operate Julie's massage parlor down on Eighth Street," she said.

"And is John Butcher one of your customers?"

"Yes, he comes weekly, sometimes twice a week," she said.

"Does your massage parlor have extra amenities for some of your regular patrons?"

"Amenities?"

"Yes, is not your place raided often for prostitution? And was John Butcher one of your guest on November 3rd of last year when a raid happened?" asked J. Morris. "Never mind, don't answer that question. Your honor, I have here the arrest record of Ms. Julie and

John Butcher caught in the very act on November 3rd 1959. Also, I have the phone appointment records showing John Butcher visits Julie's establishment two or three times a week."

"Let these items be entered into the record," said the judge, "Any further questions for this witness?"

"No, your honor."

"Mr. Milton, do you wish to question this witness?"

"No questions at this time," he said.

"You may step down," said the judge. "Mr. Higgins, call your next witness."

"The State calls Joanne Moss," said J. Morris.

After taking the oath she sat with her hands in her lap looking at the floor. "Where do you work?" asked J. Morris.

"At the State Department," she said.

"Do you know John Butcher?"

"Yes, I've had the opportunity to work with him," she said. "He's one of my bosses."

"And what kind of working relationship have you had with Mr. Butcher?"

"He's demanding, often angry and I don't know how to say this, but he has tried to force himself on me. Once he showed his privates to me when we were in a room by ourselves," she said.

"Did you encourage his behavior?"

"No, I ran out of the room and went to my desk," said Ms. Moss. "I later had my bonus cut in half. I didn't say anything. I couldn't afford to lose my job."

"Thank you, Joanne. That's all I have for you now," said J. Morris.

"Mr. Milton?" said the judge.

"Isn't it true you wear short skirts and low-cut blouses just asking for the attention of men? Have you not encouraged Mr. Butcher?"

"No sir. I do not believe I have encouraged him," said Ms. Moss.

"When you advertise your body, you can expect men will respond," said Jake Milton, as he turned and went to his seat.

"Objection," said J. Morris.

"Sustained," said Judge Parker. "Let that comment be stricken from the record."

Jake Milton hesitated. "Mr. Milton, do you have another question?" asked Judge Parker.

"No, that's all for this witness," said Jake Milton.

"We're nearing the end of the day. Court is adjourned until 8 o'clock tomorrow morning," said Judge Parker.

The courtroom emptied quickly, everyone trying to get ahead of the traffic.

The next morning, the trial commenced at exactly eight o'clock. J. Morris began by entering Jenny's letter into the record. Jake Milton objected saying a dead person could not testify. The Judge looked at the letter. "It's signed, dated, witnessed and notarized," he said. "I'll allow it."

After J. Morris read the letter aloud to the jury, he said, "This letter was given to me at the beginning of November. It clearly shows John Butcher was pursuing Virginia Anderson. She went missing at the end of November."

"Counselor, you have become your own witness," said Jake Milton, looking at J. Morris. "How do we know you just didn't make this up?"

"I was Virginia Anderson's lawyer. When I became District Attorney the court allowed me to keep some of my personal clients. Virginia Anderson was one of them," said J. Morris, addressing the judge.

"I understand," said Judge Parker. "Proceed."

"Virginia Anderson gave me the letter for safekeeping. She intended to report John Butcher to Human Recourses and thought she would be fired. She wanted prior evidence to present to the court when she sued for wrongful dismissal. It's all legal, counselor," smiling at Jake Milton.

"Call your next witness," said Judge Parker.

"I call Doctor Charles Lesh," said J. Morris. Doctor Lesh raised his right hand and took the oath. "What is your profession?"

"I'm the Montgomery County coroner," he said.

"And did you examine the body of the deceased Virginia Anderson?"

"I did."

"What did you find was the cause of death?"

"She was strangled."

"When, in your expert opinion, do you think her murder happened?"

"I believe she died somewhere around the end of November," said Doctor Lesh.

"Is there anything else you can tell us about her body?"

"Yes, we found residue under her fingernails. There's a new test, not widely used yet, called DNA. We sent the residue to Washington D.C. to be analyzed. They found it to be male human skin cells. When an arrest was made, we sent a hair from John Butcher to them. The report is back." He handed it to J. Morris. "The DNA under Virginia Anderson's fingernails matches that of John Butcher," said Doctor Lesh.

"Your honor, I would like to enter this report into the record," said J. Morris.

"Granted," said Judge Parker.

J. Morris handed the report to the stenographer and sat down.

"Mr. Milton?" motioned the judge.

"Doctor Lesh, have you ever been wrong about the date a person died?" asked Jake Milton.

"Yes, I have. And Virginia Anderson's body was badly decomposed. I could be off by a week or two," said Doctor Lesh.

"What about this DNA test. You say it's not widely used. Truth is it's not yet proven to be reliable. Am I right?"

"The test still has a few kinks to work out," said Doctor Lesh.

"Thank you, no further questions," said Jake Milton.

"We have time for one more witness before we adjourn for lunch," said Judge Parker.

"Yes sir, the State calls Sam Durham," said J. Morris. "Mr. Durham stood up and moved slowly to the witness stand, raised his right hand and took the oath.

"Mr. Durham, what is your profession?" asked J. Morris.

"I'm a fingerprint expert," he said. "I'm a sergeant with the police department."

"There was a latex glove found near Virginia Anderson's body. What can you tell me about that glove?" asked J. Morris.

"We were able to lift a fingerprint from the inside of the glove," said Sgt. Durham, smiling. "Not many people think about looking on the inside of a glove for a print."

"Do you have a match for that print?" asked J. Morris.

"Yes, sir, the print matches the index finger on the right hand of the prints we took from John Butcher," said the sergeant.

"Thank you," said J. Morris.

Jake Milton walked up to the stand and stood directly in front of Sgt. Durham.

"How long have you worked at the police department?" he asked.

"About a year and a half."

"A year and a half? That's not very long. Could you say you're not all that experienced in your field?"

"I've had the proper training. I've only been on the job for a year and a half, but I believe I have the ability to do my job," said Sgt. Durham.

"Have you ever been wrong?" asked Jake Milton.

"Yes sir, once when I first started," said Sgt. Durham.

Looking at the jury, "Then he could be wrong again," said Jake Milton.

"It was a parc____"

"That's all," interrupted Jake Milton, as he sat down.

"Court will adjourn for today," said the judge. "Have a good week-end."

Chapter 31

Jamie continued to ask about Maggie. When Stan picked Jamie up from school, he saw Maggie standing with her class., but there was no way to talk to her. That night Jamie convinced her daddy to call Maggie.

"Hello, Maggie. Jamie has been hounding me, wanting to see you. Do you think you could meet us at the park on Saturday for a while?"

"Let's make it a picnic. I know Jamie loves picnics. I'll make the sandwiches if you'll bring the chips and drinks," said Maggie. "Oh, and tell Jamie I'll bring peanut butter and jelly for her."

"Thank you, Jamie will be excited," said Brian.

It was a gorgeous fall day. The sun was bright, the sky was blue and the north wind came across the mountains to cool the air. Maggie had her sandwiches ready. She arrived at the park early, secured a table and sat gazing into space. She remembered to bring the soccer ball and wondered if Jamie still liked to play. She would try to remember to tell Brian to sign Jamie up for a community team. If he didn't have time to take her to practice and the games, Maggie was more than willing to help. Maggie pondered the connection she had with Jamie. There was just something about Jamie that was different from all her other students. Was it her cocky smile? Her ravenous energy? Her ability to reach out to those around her?

"Ms. Maggie, Ms. Maggie," shouted Jamie, as she ran into Maggie's arms.

"You've grown two inches since I've seen you," said Maggie. Brian was standing back watching.

"I'm in third grade this year. I like my teacher, but I miss my old friends."

"Maybe you can arrange to go see some of your old friends and I'm sure you'll make new friends soon," said Maggie.

"There's one girl in my reading group who talks to me. Her name is Emily," said Jamie.

"Well see there, you're making a friend already," said Maggie.

Brian sauntered up to where the girls were talking.

"Good morning," said Maggie. She made a special effort to smile. She didn't want Brian to think she was mad. Brian placed the cooler on the table and sat down on the bench beside Maggie.

"Did you bring the soccer ball?" asked Jamie.

"It's right here," said Maggie, pitching the ball in Jamie's direction. Jamie ran to retrieve it. "Come on let's play," said Jamie.

"We'll play 'keep away'" said Maggie. "Brian, get in the middle and Jamie and I will pass the ball and you try to get it. If you get it, you throw the ball and hit one of us. The person you hit has to get in the middle. The object is to keep the ball away from the person in the middle."

Brian caught the ball and hit Maggie. She went to the middle, caught the ball and bounced it off Jamie. Jamie was in the middle. The adults were tall, so they made an effort to throw the ball low. They were laughing. They were having fun. Even Brian seemed to be having a good time.

After lunch Jamie asked if she could go swing for a while, leaving Brian and Maggie alone. "Have you heard how the trial is going?" asked Maggie.

"I've snuck in a couple of times. J. Morris seems to have things under control. John Butcher is a common looking character. The more I learn about him, the more I hate him," said Brian.

"Have you been able to concentrate on your work at The Farm?" asked Maggie.

"Yes, my boss who has been my friend for years has helped me, but he's resigning. I've decided to apply for his job. With Jamie back home I can't be running off to foreign countries trying to solve international cases. My job is dangerous. It's not fair to her," said Brian.

"I thought you were just helping J. Morris with the drug case and I know you've done some work on Jenny's case," said Maggie.

"It's more complicated than that," said Brian.

"I would ask how, but you've told me not to ask questions, so I won't," said Maggie.

"If I get the job at The Farm, I may be able to tell you more," said Brian.

"When will you know if you've got the job?" asked Maggie.

"They'll take applications for another two weeks and then I should know," said Brian.

Jamie came running back and sat down between Brian and Maggie, putting her head on Maggie's shoulder. "I love you," she said. Maggie looked at Brian. "I love you, too," she said, giving Jamie a little squeeze. It was nice just sitting in the cool fall air, relaxed with cares far away. Maggie looked down. Jamie's eyes were closed. She had fallen asleep. Maggie closed her eyes and snuggled closer to Jamie.

She could think of nothing she loved more.

Brian took the soccer ball and kicked it around on the grass before he came back and stretched out on the bench to take his nap.

It was three o'clock when they left the park. "If you see me at school, wave," said Maggie. "And, we'll do this again real soon."

"I will," said Jamie. "Maybe next time we can bring Paula along to play with us."

"That's a great idea. Brian do you still have Paula's telephone number? Maybe you can call her mother and see if she would like to come with us to the park in a couple of weeks?"

"I'll check into it," said Brian.

Chapter 32

At eight o'clock Monday morning the judge was banging his gavel and declaring court in session. The foreman of the jury stood. "Sir may I have a word with you?"

"Yes, approach the bench," said Judge Parker.

"Sir, two of our jury members have reported to me they have received anonymous threating calls. I don't know what it means, but I thought I should tell you," said the foreman.

"Thank you," said the judge. He banged the gavel again. "Circumstances concerning this trial have made it necessary to sequester the jury." The jury looked surprised and uneasy. "You will not be allowed to go home today. The bailiff will call your family and they'll bring you a change of clothes. You will not be allowed to talk with anyone outside this court. Do not read the papers or watch TV. You may talk among yourselves, but with no one else," said the judge.

One of the men on the jury raised his hand. "Sir, my wife is a nurse and works at night. We have three children. If I have to spend the night here my children will be left alone. What can I do?"

"You are excused," said Judge Parker. "Alternate number one will take your place. Does everyone understand what's happening? You'll be assigned roommates. Your clothes will arrive tonight. Dinner will be served in the dining hall by inmates. The food is usually pretty good. I hope you'll be comfortable." No one asked any questions although they were all a little stunned. The alternate took her place in the jury box and the juror she replaced left for home.

"We'll take a thirty-minute break so the bailiff can get phone numbers and make a list of the clothes you want your family to bring to you," said the judge. The jury members gathered around the bailiff. He handed the information to a secretary who proceeded to make the necessary phone calls.

The judge came back to the bench and the bailiff called the court back into session.

"Prosecutor, call your next witness," said Judge Parker.

"The state calls George Anderson," said J. Morris. George came from the back of the room to take the oath.

"Mr. Anderson, where do you live?"

"I live at Pilot Ridge," said George Anderson.

"And for the jury that doesn't know where Pilot Ridge is, tell us where Pilot Ridge is located," said J. Morris.

"Pilot Ridge is in the foothills of the Appalachian Mountains. It used to be Hoot Ridge before the plane crashed up there. The pilot jumped out of the plane and came floating down from the sky. It was a sight of see. After that they called it Pilot Ridge," said George Anderson.

"Objection. Interesting story, but what does that have to do with the location of Pilot Ridge?" asked Jake Milton.

"I just thought you might want to know," said George.

"Mr. Anderson, stick to the relevant facts," said Judge Parker.

"Yes sir, said George.

"How far is Salt Creek from your house?"

"About a mile," said George Anderson.

"Do you know John Butcher?"

"Yes, he has been going coon hunting with me and some of the fellows," said George Anderson.

"Does he often come to your house?"

"No, sir, I reckon he's only been to my house twice," said George.

"And when did he come to your house?" asked J. Morris.

"I believe it was the last week in November. I don't know the exact date," said George. "And there was another time. I don't remember the date."

"Why did he come to your house?"

"He brought me a redbone hound. But it didn't seem right. Reverend Robert Jones was there with him," said George.

"Thank you, no further questions at this time," said J. Morris.

"Mr. Milton," said the judge.

"What did you think about the present John Butcher brought you?" asked Jake Milton.

"I liked the dog. He's a pretty good hunter. He won second place at the time trials last May. I was right proud of him," said George.

"Do you consider John Butcher to be a friend?" asked Jake Milton.

"I guess I did at the time, but now I don't know. If he killed my daughter. . .

"Your daughter?"

"Yes, sir, she has lived in Durant for several years. We didn't visit much. Not many people put us together, but she was my girl," said George.

"I'm sorry for your loss," said Jake Milton, as he sat down.

John Butcher leaned over and whispered in Jake Milton's ear. "I didn't know he had a daughter," he said.

"This is not good," whispered Jake Milton.

"Call your next witness," said Judge Parker.

"The State calls Reverend Robert Jones to the stand," said J. Morris.

"Do you swear to tell the truth, the whole truth and nothing but the truth?" asked the bailiff.

"I do," said Robby Jones.

"Were you with John Butcher the night he took the redbone hound to George Anderson?" asked J. Morris.

"I didn't go there with him. I met him there," said Robby.

"Why did you meet him there?"

"He asked me to pick up and bring a crate of drugs that had been dropped near the Jungle," said Robby.

"Were you accustomed to transporting drugs for John Butcher?"

"That was the first time. He usually picked them up when he went hunting," said Robby.

"Were you arrested for drug possession about two months ago?"

"Yes, sir, I don't take drugs myself. I was reselling them," said Robby.

"And, was there a reason you were selling drugs for John Butcher?" asked J. Morris.

"Objection" shouted Jake Milton, "leading the witness."

"I'll restate. Was there a reason you were selling drugs?" asked J. Morris.

"Yes, John Butcher threatened to take my children away from me if I didn't," said Robby.

"What did John Butcher have to do with your children?" asked J. Morris.

"My wife and I couldn't have children. John Butcher helped us get our children. They came from Guatemala. He helped us adopt," said Robby.

"Thank you," said J. Morris.

Jake Milton rose and slowly walked over to stand in front of Reverend Jones.

"Reverend Jones, you were arrested for transporting drugs for resell. You are a known felon. Why should we believe you when you tell us you were transporting drugs for John Butcher? Weren't you transporting drugs to sell for your own financial gain?" asked Jake Milton.

"No sir. I never made a dime. I was trying to protect my family. And you should believe me because I'm telling the truth," said Reverend Jones.

"We'll adjourn for the day," said Judge Parker. "We'll be back tomorrow at eight a.m. "I hope the jury will have a pleasant evening. The bailiff will be in the hallway. If you need something, he'll be glad to help you."

"All rise," said the bailiff, as the jury filed out to find their rooms.

Chapter 33

The bailiff woke the jury at 6:00 a.m. Breakfast was at seven. Court convened at eight. There was no time to waste.

"Are you ready to begin," asked Judge Parker, looking at J. Morris Higgins.

"Yes, sir, I have an affidavit from Avery Sutton. He has had bypass surgery and is unable to be in court, your honor," said J. Morris.

"Please read the affidavit," said Judge Parker.

After reading Avery Sutton's statement, J. Morris submitted it for the records. Jake Milton did not object.

"Call your next witness," said the judge.

"The State calls Mark James to the stand."

"Mr. James, what is your profession?"

"I work for the Federal Aviation Association in Washington D. C.," he said.

"I only have one question for you, who owns the plane that Mr. Sutton saw dumping drugs?"

"Well, the plane is owned by Butcher Agriculture Corporation, headed by John Butcher," said Mr. James.

"How do you know it's the same plane?"

"The N-number matches the suspected plane's number where the drugs were found," said Mr. James.

"Thank you," said J. Morris.

"Defense?"

"Would it be possible for someone to use the plane without my client's knowledge?" asked Jake Milton.

"I guess it would be possible," said Mr. James.

"Then we can't be certain of how the drugs got in the plane or who put them there, can we?" said Jake Milton.

"I guess not," said Mr. James.

"No further questions," said Jake Milton, as he sat down.

"We call Ken Douglas," said J. Morris. He came forward and took the oath.

"Mr. Douglas, what do you do for a living?"

"I'm a pilot," he said.

"Did you get arrested for possession of drugs found on your Cessna 182B Skylane?"

"Yes," said the pilot.

"Who owns that plane? Or better still, who writes your paycheck?" asked J. Morris.

"My paycheck comes from Butcher Agriculture Corporation," said Mr. Douglas.

"Thank you. Your witness," he said, looking at Jake Milton.

"Did you ever hear the name John Butcher before this trial?"

"No sir."

"So, in truth, you don't know the person who writes your check, do you?"

"I don't know," said the pilot.

"Thank you," said Jake Milton, "No further questions."

"You may step down, next witness," said the judge.

"The State calls Steve Max," said J. Morris. Steve looked agitated. He had driven all night from Mobile Alabama to be in court. He yawned as he sat down.

"Where do you work?"

"I head up the business at the Port of Mobile," said Mr. Max.

"Do you receive crates from the Butcher Agricultural Corporation in Mexico?"

"Yes."

"And have they ever been known to contain drugs?"

"Yes, we inspect crates at random and drugs have been found several times over the past year," said Mr. Max.

"Did you report your finding to the authorities?"

"Yes, it is my understanding there was never enough evidence to pursue the case," said Mr. Max.

"Why do you think this is true?" asked J. Morris.

"I can't tell you for sure. But I think maybe somebody is being paid off," said Mr. Max.

"Speculation! Move to strike," said Jake Milton.

"Stick to what you know," said the judge. "Strike that statement from the record."

"No more questions," said J. Morris. "Thank you,

Jake Milton stepped up to the stand. "Did you see my client put drugs in a crate?

"No."

"How would you know if my client had anything to do with those drugs?"

"I wouldn't," said Mr. Max.

"Thank you, no further questions," said Jake Milton.

"Call you next witness," said Judge Parker.

"The Prosecution rests," said J. Morris.

"We'll break for lunch and the defense will present their case beginning at 2 o'clock," said the judge.

The jury went to the cafeteria for lunch. It was another fantastic meal prepared by the inmates from The Farm.

Two o'clock was upon them. The jury had little time to relax. They were anxious to hear what John Butcher's lawyer would have to say.

"Mr. Milton, call your first witness," said Judge Parker.

"Your honor, I want to recall Ken Douglas to the stand."

"Mr. Douglas, you are still under oath," said the bailiff.

"Yes sir," said Ken Douglas.

"Mr. Douglas, how did you get your job working for the Butcher Agriculture Corporation?" asked Jake Milton.

"There was an advertisement in the newspaper for a pilot and an address where I could send an application. I sent in my application and they contacted me by phone," said Ken Douglas.

"Who contacted you by phone?"

"His name was Juan Rodriguez," said Ken Douglas.

"What did he say you would be doing?" asked Jake Milton. "In other words what would your job be like?"

"He said I would pick up crates of agricultural products from the Port of Mobile and take them to different places in the southern United States," said Ken Douglas. "He said I shouldn't ask too many questions, just follow orders. The pay was really good, so I just followed orders. I had no idea about what I was delivering."

"Was there ever a time when you got an order from Senator Butcher?"

"No sir, I had never heard of him until this trial," said Ken Douglas.

"Thank you. Your witness," he said, looking at J. Morris.

"No questions," said J. Morris.

"Call your next witness," said Judge Parker.

"The defense calls Tom Stem to the stand," said Jake Milton. Tom raised his right hand and took the oath. "Tom, where do you work?"

"In human resources at the State Department," said Tom.

"How long have you worked there?" asked Jake Milton.

"About six years."

"Where did you work before the State Department?"

"I was unemployed for almost two years when my friend John Butcher came through for me. He got me the job. He's a true friend. You can count on him when you have a need. I've never met anyone as thoughtful as he is," said Tom Stem.

"Thank you," said Jake Milton.

"Mr. Higgins?" said the judge.

"Yes sir. Tom, has John Butcher ever needed anything from you?"

"No, not a thing," said Tom Stem.

"Just wait," said J. Morris.

"Objection," said Jake Milton. You're badgering the witness."

"Counselor, refrain from making snide comments," said Judge Parker.

"Yes sir," said J. Morris, as Mr. Stem went back to his seat.

"Call your next witness," said the judge.

"I call Eileen Baxter," said Jake Milton. Eileen was a short little woman with red hair. She smiled at Jake Milton as he approached the witness stand.

"What is your profession, Mrs. Baxter?"

"I'm the church secretary at Montgomery Baptist Church," she said.

"How do you know my client?"

"He's a member of our church. I see him almost every Sunday," said Mrs. Baxter.

"Do you hear about most of the things that happen at your church?"

"Yes, people tell me things (confidential things) and I'm here to tell you everything I hear about John Butcher is good. He's a hard worker in the church and out of the church, too. People praise him to 'high heaven'," said Eileen Baxter.

"Thank you, no more questions," said Jake Milton.

"Mr. Higgins?" said the judge.

"No questions, your honor," said J. Morris.

John Butcher and Jake Milton were in a huddle. There seemed to be a disagreement. "Yes," yelled John Butcher, red faced and tense. Jake Milton stepped back. "I call John Butcher to the stand," he said.

John Butcher raised his right hand. "Do you swear to tell the truth, the whole truth and nothing but the truth?" asked the bailiff.

"I do," said John Butcher.

"You may be seated," said Judge Parker.

"Do you have a business by the name of Butcher Agriculture Corporation in Juarez Mexico?" asked Jake Milton.

"Yes, I have several business interests around the world," said John Butcher, smiling.

"Do you attend to these businesses personally?"

"I go to Mexico two or three times a year," said John Butcher.

"Do you know Juan Rodriguez, the man who hired Ken Douglas?" asked Jake Milton.

"I have trouble with Mexican names. I know there's some Mexican fellow that runs the place down there," said John Butcher.

"Do you have any knowledge of drugs being shipped in Butcher Agricultural Corporation crates to the United States?" asked Jake Milton.

"Not a clue," said John Butcher, smiling.

"And did you know Ken Douglas was delivering products from your company?"

"I didn't know Mr. Douglas was delivering. I knew somebody was. The company was operating smoothly," said John Butcher. "The produce was being delivered."

"What kind of produce was being delivered?"

"All kinds of agricultural produce such as peppers and tomatoes. At other times blankets and sometimes trinkets," said Butcher.

"Let's switch to Pilot Ridge. Did Reverend Robert Jones deliver drugs to you the night you brought the redbone hound to George Anderson?"

"No," he said with emphasis.

"Then why did you ask Reverend Jones to meet you there?"

"He goes hunting with the fellows and I wanted to show him the new hound," said John Butcher. There was a shuffling in the back of the court and a loud whisper from Reverend Jones, "That's a lie," he said. "We didn't even look at the dog."

"Order in the court," said Judge Parker, banging his gavel.

"How do you see yourself in regards to visiting Ms. Julie's massage parlor?"

"I'm a busy man and I'm not getting any younger. I need a massage to keep me going. The last time I checked, it's not illegal to get a massage," said John Butcher.

"How do you account for having your fingerprint inside a glove found in the woods near Salt Creek?" asked Jake Milton.

"I hunt in those woods and one time I used a pair of gloves when I skinned a coon," said John Butcher. "I should have thrown that glove in the trash. I plead guilty to littering."

"Thank you," said Jake Milton.

J. Morris stood directly in front of John Butcher, looking intensely into his eyes. "Mr. Butcher, what kind of agricultural products did you say your company ships from Mexico?"

"Mostly fruits and vegetables," said Butcher.

"Do you consider heroin to be a fruit or vegetable?" asked J. Morris.

"Certainly not," said Butcher.

"But you do admit drugs have been found in crates that come from your company?" said J. Morris.

"I don't know how that happened," said John Butcher.

Senator Butcher, how is it your ex-wife finds you to be angry and out of control when so many others think you are kind and helpful?" asked J. Morris.

"Everyone is entitled to their own opinion," said John Butcher.

"Isn't it true your anger comes from suppressed sexual desires?" said J. Morris.

"Well, now he's a psychologist," said John Butcher.

"Isn't it true that's the reason you visit the so-called massage parlor? Isn't it true when you pay for sex you are not criticized? Isn't it true you're a little man and size matters?"

"Objection, objection," shouted Jake Milton.

"Counselor, counselor," said the judge. John Butcher was red in the face and shaking.

"Yes, sir Judge" said J. Morris, knowing he was pushing his boundaries.

"When you called Reverend Jones and asked him to meet you at the Anderson's home, isn't it true you wanted a witness to confer with you because in fact you had just taken a young woman by force to a secluded spot hoping to have sex with her and when she refused you killed Virginia Anderson and dumped her body in Salt Creek?"

"No, no," said John Butcher. "No."

"Isn't it true, you strangled her and decided to take her far away from Durant to the mountains where you thought no one would ever find her? You needed an excuse to be there so you brought the dog to George Anderson?" said J. Morris.

"Did you bring the dog in your car? Why not your truck?"

"I drive my car almost as much as I drive my truck," said John Butcher.

"The smell of the dog is still in your car and the smell of Virginia Anderson's perfume lingers in the trunk of your car. You had no way of knowing you had killed George's daughter. You did kill his daughter, didn't you?" said J. Morris.

John Butcher stood, shaking, wringing his hands and floundering, tears running down his face, "No, no, no, I didn't mean to kill her. She was so beautiful. I loved her. I wanted her to love me. She defied me. She wouldn't let me touch her. She said she hated me. I couldn't help it. I grabbed her. She fought me. I fought back. I couldn't help it. I just wanted her to love me," said John Butcher, crying and clinging to the rail.

"Your honor, I need a recess," said Jake Milton.

"We'll take a thirty-minute break," said Judge Parker.

The courtroom emptied quickly. No one was talking. The energy in the room had dissipated. Jake Milton accepted the judge's offer to use his office for a conference during the recess.

When it was time to reconvene a tense silence filled the room as the judge entered the room and banged his gavel. Even Judge Parker was somber.

"Mr. Milton, do you have another witness?"

"No sir, the defense rest," said Jake Milton.

"This court will meet again tomorrow at eight o'clock when we'll hear closing arguments. Have a good night," said Judge Parker.

The guards came for John Butcher, handcuffed him and took him back to his cell.

The Farm

When Stan entered his office, he heard his phone ringing. He rushed in to answer it.

"Hello," he said.

"You're not going to believe this," said J. Morris. "The pervert just confessed to killing Jenny."

"What?"

"Right there on the witness stand. He broke down and cried and said it was an accident. He didn't mean to kill her," said J. Morris.

"I can't believe it. It's over," said Stan.

"Well, it's not over yet. We've still got closing arguments and the jury will decide his fate," said J. Morris.

"Still, I feel relieved," said Stan.

"I'll keep in touch," said J. Morris, as he hung up the phone.

Jeff was standing in the door. "What're you relieved about?" he asked.

"I just heard. John Butcher confessed to killing Jenny," said Stan.

"That's a relief," said Jeff. "Maybe now you can begin to heal."

"Just knowing helps," said Stan. "I haven't been able to think about anything else. I haven't even told anyone about my new job."

"It'll be yours tomorrow," said Jeff. "I'm winding things down. We'll have a little going away party tonight. I brought you the keys to my office. I know you'll do an excellent job. You've already been taking care of most everything," said Jeff. "Will I see you tonight?"

"I wouldn't miss it. And, I intend to come to Florida, too. You're not going to get rid of me," said Stan.

"I hope we can stay in touch. I'll miss seeing you. We'll talk. Florida's not that far away," said Jeff.

"We've touched on this before, but I'm just going to come right out and say it: I really don't like the way the doctors have been treating the patients—drying them out and readdicting them, just so they can try something different. I hope to make some changes," said Stan.

"What happens after I'm gone is on you," said Jeff. "You have my contact information. Call me anytime. I'll be there to listen and you know me, I'm always ready to give advice," giving Stan a pat on the shoulder, as he left.

Stan wanted to tell Maggie, but should he? Would she feel like he was using her as a crutch, always coming to her with his troubles? No, this wasn't trouble. He would just be sharing news, better coming from him than her hearing it on the TV and she would want to know.

"Maggie, it's Brian. I thought you would want to know, John Butcher confessed to killing Jenny."

"I thought it was him," said Maggie. "How did it happen?"

"J. Morris called. I guess he asked the right questions. John Butcher broke down right there on the witness stand and said he killed her by accident," said Brian.

"It sounds like things are coming to a close," said Maggie.

"Yes, I feel relieved; sad, but relieved," said Brian. "Oh, I have some good news. I got the job at The Farm."

"That's wonderful. Now you can spend more time with Jamie," said Maggie.

"The job begins tomorrow. I really hate to see Jeff go," said Brian.

"Maybe you and Jamie can visit him in Florida," said Maggie.

"Yes, we'll certainly do that," said Brian. "How's your daddy doing?"

"He's doing well. I haven't seen him in two weeks because I've been busy with school, but he and Mother are coming down here on Saturday. Mother said she's driving. She still doesn't trust him to drive," said Maggie, laughing.

"We really enjoyed the picnic," said Brian. "Jamie couldn't quit talking about it."

"I enjoyed it, too. It was a nice relaxing day. I think we all needed it," said Maggie.

"Well, guess I'd better get off the phone, go home and figure out what I'm going to make Jamie for dinner. You know for some reason that question comes up every evening. Jamie's not too fond of my cooking," laughed Brian. "Thank God she likes grilled cheese sandwiches."

"You've got to learn how to make vegetables," said Maggie. "You don't want a child with malnutrition."

"I think I'll make mac and cheese out of a box and green beans out of a can tonight. I'll try to do better," said Brian. "Got to go, Jamie will be home from school soon. We've got a carpool going. I drive the girls to school and Paula's mom picks them up. It's good for Jamie. She feels like she's more a part of things. Talk to you later. Bye."

"Bye," said Maggie, feeling a little jealous that she wasn't the one helping with Jamie.

Chapter 34

The night seemed short. It was time to be back in court. J. Morris hoped his closing statement would be sufficient. Jake Milton looked a little haggled. John Butcher sat unresponsive, looking at his hands.

"All rise," said the bailiff. Judge Parker entered the courtroom, sat down and banged his gavel. "You may be seated," he said. "Mr. Higgins are you ready with your final statement?"

"Yes sir," said J. Morris.

"Ladies and gentlemen of the jury, you have patiently listened to testimony after testimony all week. John Butcher knew he killed Virginia Anderson, and was guilty of this heinous crime, but he didn't confess until we had him between a rock and a hard place. He pursued Virginia Anderson alarming her to the degree that she left a written statement with her lawyer because she thought if she defied him much longer, he would have her fired. She never dreamed he would kill her. He not only killed her but disposed of her body in a creek bed in the middle of a jungle in a place where he thought she would never be found. He said he loved her. John Butcher is a sick man. Is that what you do to someone you love; brutally strangle her and leave her body to decay? John Butcher is guilty by his own admission. John Butcher killed Virginia Anderson. You will decide his fate."

The men and women of the jury were attentive and listening. J. Morris walked back and forth in front of them.

"John Butcher has been a busy man. What about his responsibility for the drugs coming into our state? It's his corporation that's sending them here and his airplane that's dropping them in your neighborhoods. The defense will want you to believe he is innocent, that he is unaware of the drug activity, but that is not true. We have presented witnesses who have delivered drugs to Senator Butcher and who have sold drugs for him. He is responsible. And he must be held responsible. Again, you must decide. Thank you," said J. Morris.

"Mr. Milton," said Judge Parker.

"My client has confessed to killing Virginia Anderson. She led him on to the point where he believed she was fond of him. He fell in love with her. When she refused his affections, they struggled and he accidently killed her. He didn't mean to kill her. He was emotionally disturbed by her rejection and lost control of his actions. John Butcher is a good man that has helped many people in his lifetime. He cares about people and he loved Virginia Anderson."

Jake Milton moved to the other side of the jury box and put his hands in his pockets.

"You cannot hold him responsible for all of his business interests. He must leave the day-to-day operations to other people. He can't possibly know all that's happening everywhere and there is absolutely no proof he was aware of, much less involved in, drug trafficking. You might say what about Reverend Jones testimony? Reverend Jones is a known drug pusher and he was arrested and sent to The Farm. The only reason he was released early was because the prosecution wanted him to testify against John Butcher. It's the convicted felon Reverend Jones's word against the upstanding senator's word, John Butcher. You heard the testimonies of people praising John Butcher for his generosity. His fate is in your hands. Don't let him down. He's depending on you. Thank you."

"Mr. Higgins, rebuttal?" asked the judge.

"There's two sides to John Butcher. Yes, he's known for his light and bright generosity, but his underside is as black as coal. He's a murderer and he's a drug lord. It's up to you to find him guilty, to put an end to his shady dealings. Thank you."

"This ends the trial," said Judge Parker, addressing the jury. "John Butcher has confessed to Virginia Anderson's murder; therefore, he is guilty. You must decide if he's guilty of murder 1 or murder 2. To find him guilty of first-degree murder you must agree he planned or premeditated to kill Virginia Anderson, or if he forced her to be with him committing a felony before he killed her. To find him guilty of second-degree murder you must agree that the defendant did not plan Virginia Anderson's murder, but acted in a way he knew could cause her death. In the matter of drug trafficking, you must believe that John Butcher knew and participated in the act of drug trafficking and is guilty beyond a reasonable doubt. The jury will retire to the conference room for deliberations. Please notify the bailiff when you reach a verdict. We will reconvene at that time."

"All rise," said the bailiff. The jury followed the foreman to the conference room. The guard came for John Butcher. The lawyers packed up their papers and headed back to their offices. Now, all they could do was wait.

The Farm

There had been no good-bye party, no cake, no friend's congratulations. People at The Farm thought Stan had been promoted to a higher position. After all, he was moving to the corner office. Truth was, he was stepping down from a prestigious position and was taking a cut in pay. Few people knew, and they were not allowed to talk about it. (All of the undercover CIA Agents activities were covert and clandestine.)

Surrounded by files and trash, Stan sat in his office starring at the picture of Jenny and Jamie on his desk. Maintenance would come tomorrow and move whatever he wanted to take to the new office.

Stan picked up the file containing pictures of the coon dog trials. Recruiting Junior was an accomplishment he could be proud of. He couldn't say that about all his missions.

After graduating from Kentucky State University in 1947 with a major in Criminal Justice and a minor in Spanish, Stan joined the newly formed Central Intelligence Agency. He trained for a year in Washington D. C. before he was sent on his first assignment to Guatemala for three months. The Guatemalan Revolution was thought to be funded by the communist party because their President had legalized the Communist Guatemalan Party of Labor. It was 1953 before Stan realized how the United States had drawn exaggerated conclusions about the extent of communism in the Guatemalan government. President Eisenhower was bent on having Arbenz relieved of his position. Stan found himself heading up the United States unit that produced psychological warfare in the form of radio announcements and leaflets that intimidated the Guatemalan army and eventually led to Arbenz's resignation.

Stan opened the file drawer where he kept his credentials locked away. Tomorrow he would no longer need them. He took a match from his cigarette holder and struck it. The flames rushed up the paper as one by one the documents were turned into ashes.

Looking back, Stan wondered what had been accomplished. He had been taught to do his job and ask few questions. Now that he was leaving, he wondered just what he had given up to be at the bidding of the CIA.

In 1948 while home on leave he met and married Jenny. She accepted his CIA lifestyle. He was home three months and gone three. She knew not to ask questions.

Stan continued to read through files. He smiled when he came across a picture of the Dalai Lama. He remembered in 1950 how he had arranged for the Dalai Lama to receive a large sum of money to be used by the Tibetan government to lobby for international support against China. He had enjoyed the time he spent with the Dalai Lama. At the time his head was shaved and he had a full beard. He answered to the name of Max Tanner.

In 1952, when Jamie was born, life became more complicated. He and Jenny were fortunate to have their next-door neighbor, Ms. Jarvis, to look after Jamie. She knew him only as Stan Turner and he gave her an emergency phone number. In spite of his job, he wanted to protect his daughter. Ms. Jarvis passed away shortly after Stan returned home. *Another loss for Jamie*, thought Stan.

Stan was in Vietnam when he was called to report to his superior officer. He was under cover as a Second Lieutenant. His hair was dyed black, with a butch haircut. The sun had darkened his skin and he spoke with a Spanish accident. He had just completed an assignment to prevent the Viet Cong troops from entering South Vietnam. He had facilitated the placement of listening devices to track their movements along a northern trail.

When he was boarding the helicopter to report to headquarters, one of the sergeants came up to him and said, "Sir, I was told to report to you. Three of our men were killed last night by the Viet Cong in a raid on their living quarters. He didn't ask their names. But now he wished he had. The circumstances were just too similar. Maggie must never know.

"You have an emergency at home. You must leave immediately," said the sergeant.

"What kind of emergency?" asked the lieutenant.

"Sir, I wasn't given the details. I was told you need to report home right away," said the sergeant. Stan left immediately not knowing what he would find at home and knowing his mission in Vietnam had failed.

When Stan was home, he found out from Ms. Jarvis that Jamie was still with her and it had been over a week since she had seen

Jenny. That's when Stan realized Jenny was missing. He took Jamie to his parents' home in Missouri and began his search for Jenny.

He was debriefed by the CIA. He would never be allowed to discuss his CIA missions and his appearance was altered once again. There was only a handful of people who knew who he was.

After two weeks he decided one parent was better than none. He brought Jamie home, changed their names and her school. He would do his best to protect her. His new assignment was working undercover on the drug problem in Durant.

The past year had changed his life. Maggie had changed his life. Today was the start of a new way of living, a new way of thinking— a new beginning.

Chapter 35

The jury had taken three days to reach their verdict and now they were back. J. Morris called Stan. "If you want to come to court and hear the verdict in person you should come at 10:00 a. m. The jury stayed out a long time. I'm a little worried. I'm not exactly sure what's going to happen," said J. Morris.

"I'll be there," said Stan.

Stan arrived at the courtroom and sat in the back. The judge and jury took their places. Judge Parker banged his gavel and declared the court in session. "Has the jury reached a verdict?" asked Judge Parker.

"Yes, your honor," said the foreman.

"The defendant will rise," said Judge Parker. "What is your verdict?"

"On the count of drug trafficking, not guilty," said the foreman. A rumble went up in the courtroom. Judge Parker banged his gavel. "Order," he said. "And, on the second count?"

"On the count of murder, we found John Butcher guilty of second-degree murder," said the foreman.

The judge poled each juror and each concurred with the verdict. "The sentence hearing will be tomorrow at 8:00 a.m." said Judge Parker. "Jury, thank you for your service. You are released from duty. This court is now adjourned."

J. Morris caught up with Stan. "I can't believe they let him off the drug charge," said J. Morris.

"At any rate he's charged with Jenny's murder. He'll go away for a long time," said Stan.

"I sure hope so," said J. Morris, who was beginning to feel a little unsure about John Butcher's future.

It was the following day. John Butcher would be sentenced. The morning light brought anxiety. Stan wondered what sentence John Butcher would receive. Surely Judge Parker would send him away. His cunning personality and high position would not fool Judge

Parker. Stan couldn't stay away. He had to go to the courtroom one more time.

"Order in the court," said Judge Parker as he banged his gavel. "We're here today to sentence John Butcher for the murder of Virginia Anderson. Mr. Butcher please stand." John Butcher and his attorney, Jake Milton, stood. "After careful consideration, I hereby sentence you to fifteen years at Green Meadow Mental Institution," said Judge Parker.

John Butcher looked surprised. Jake Milton smiled.

Stan stalked out of the courtroom.

Chapter 36

Saturday morning Lucy and Avery arrived at Maggie's house around 10:30 a.m. Maggie had made a roast, potatoes and carrots for lunch. It appeared they would have a calm relaxed day. Lucy prattled on about having to drive so far and how her back was hurting. Avery was quiet.

"How are you feeling?" asked Maggie.

"I'm awful tired," said Avery.

"What have you been doing," asked Maggie.

"Not much, the neighbors are still taking care of my animals for me," said Avery.

"It's really good when you have friends to help," said Maggie.

"Speaking of friends, whatever happened with my coon hunting buddy, John Butcher?" asked Avery. "I know somebody said he was arrested for drug trafficking. That's hard for me to believe. He seemed like a pretty good fellow."

Maggie was standing looking out the window. "Well, Daddy, you may have trouble believing this, but yesterday in court John Butcher broke down and confessed to killing George and Martha Anderson's daughter. He said it was an accident and he loved her, but he dumped her body in Salt Creek hoping nobody would ever find it. He didn't know she was George's daughter," said Maggie. Maggie turned to look at her daddy. Avery was clutching his chest and gasping for air.

"Daddy, Daddy," screamed Maggie. "What's wrong? Mother, come here, quick."

Lucy came running in spilling her coffee. "What's the matter?" she asked, failing to see Avery.

"We've got to get Daddy to the emergency room," said Maggie. "He's having another heart attack."

Lucy put her coffee down and began to cry. "Why is this happening to me?" she whined.

"Mother, stay calm," said Maggie. "Get on one side of Daddy and I'll get on the other. We have to get him in the car. Stop crying and help me."

Lucy tried to focus. They finally got Avery in the car. Maggie drove like she had never driven before, lights on and horn blaring, until a siren and flashing lights came in behind her. She pulled over. "Officer, my daddy's having a heart attack," she yelled out the window.

"Follow me," said the officer, as he pulled out in front of Maggie. He led her through red lights and stop signs into the emergency room parking lot. He jumped out of his car and ran in to the emergency room and brought a wheelchair back, wheeled Avery in and alerted the emergency room staff. Avery was immediately in the treatment room. Maggie and Lucy had to stay in the waiting room. Maggie looked up and saw Brian coming in the door. She ran into his arms, sobbing. "Daddy is having another heart attack," she said. "How did you know?"

"I heard the policeman on my shortwave radio. I had a feeling it might be you so I drove by your house. Your car was gone and your parents' car was in the driveway. Your front door was standing wide open. I turned the lock, closed the door and came directly to the hospital," said Brian.

"I don't know, I'm so afraid he won't make it," said Maggie, clinging to Brian.

"You've got to be strong for your daddy," said Brian. "Think positive thoughts. Send him your energy." Lucy was sitting dumbfounded. Maggie and Brian sat down beside her. The doctor came out to talk with them.

"Your daddy has had a major heart attack. How long ago did he have bypass surgery?"

"It's been about two months now," said Maggie.

"His heart is only functioning at 30% right now. That makes him very fragile. I'm going to admit him to the hospital so we can keep an eye on him. He can live with 30% function, but he will have to be very careful. He'll have to curtail his activity and rest most of the time. He will not survive another heart attack," said the doctor.

"When can we see him?" asked Maggie. Lucy was still quiet. She hadn't said a word since they arrived in the emergency room.

"You can go in now, one at a time. Try not to excite him. He needs to stay calm," said the doctor.

"Mother do you want to go first?" asked Maggie.

"What? No, you go," said Lucy.

Maggie looked at Brian. "You go," he said. "I'll stay here with your mom."

Maggie followed the doctor into the exam room. Avery was pale and shaking, looking like he was half asleep. "Daddy its Maggie, you gave us a scare," she said.

"I'm just so tired," said Avery.

"I know," said Maggie. "They're going to admit you to the hospital so they can keep an eye on you for a while."

"The doctor told me," said Avery. "I'm alright with that. I need watching over, I guess."

"Don't you worry about anything. I'll take care of Mother and we'll see what needs to be done back at the house," said Maggie.

"I know you will," said Avery, as he closed his eyes and dropped off to sleep. Maggie tiptoed out.

"Mother, I told Daddy we'll take care of things. He doesn't have to worry," said Maggie. "He's asleep. Go in and sit with him. It'll be good for him if he wakes up and sees you there."

Lucy made her way to the exam room and sat down beside Avery's bed. She reached for his hand.

Maggie and Brian sat in the waiting room holding hands. Maggie couldn't imagine what she would do without Brian. He was the first one she thought of when she needed help. He was the first person she thought of when she had good news to share. He was the one she could talk to.

"I'm so glad you're here," said Maggie.

"I'm happy to be here," said Brian. "I had to be here."

The nurse moved Avery up to a hospital room. Lucy went with him. Brian and Maggie went to the car to talk. "I don't know where our relationship is going, but I know I want to be near you," said Brian.

"It feels right when I'm with you," said Maggie.

"Maybe it's time for us to have our date," said Brian.

"I don't feel much like going dancing," said Maggie. "Not while Daddy's so critical."

"Let's just go out to dinner," said Brian. "But Jamie might have to come along. I don't have anybody to leave her with. I don't know. I might be able to arrange for her to have a sleepover with Paula. Let me see what I can do."

"Where's Jamie today?" asked Maggie.

"She's at Paula's house. They're inseparable. I'm really glad Jamie has a good friend," said Brian.

"Me too," said Maggie. "Little girls really need girlfriends."

"Jamie loves you. She counts you as being her very best girlfriend," said Brian.

"We're joined at the heart," said Maggie. "I had better get myself up and take Mother back to my house. She may want to go home. I may have to go to Boonetown tonight," said Maggie.

"I'll pick Jamie up and meet you back at your house and go with you if you take her home," said Brian.

"Thank you," said Maggie. "I'm really tired. It'll help a lot to have the two of you go with me."

"Alright then, I'll see you there," said Brian, reaching over giving Maggie a kiss on the cheek.

Maggie hurried to her daddy's room. "Mother, do you want to go back to my house or should I take you home?"

"Our car is at your house. You can follow me home. I don't like being out at night by myself," said Lucy. "Maybe it's time for me to quit work and stay home with your daddy."

"I think that's a good idea. It's not like you need the money," said Maggie, as she and Lucy began driving back to Maggie's house.

Brian and Jamie arrived at the house about the same time as Lucy and Maggie. "Brian and Jamie are going with me to keep me company on the way back," said Maggie.

"Good, your daddy would worry if he knew you were out at night by yourself," said Lucy.

It was just turning dark by the time Lucy was safely home. Maggie was thankful for Brian and Jamie. Brian insisted on driving. Maggie laid her head back on the headrest and fell asleep. Jamie went to sleep in the backseat. Brian was happy taking care of his girls.

Chapter 37

"How would you like to have dinner with Ms. Maggie?"

"Yes, yes, can we?" said Jamie.

"I'll call her and see if she can go," said Stan.

"Maggie, how about if Jamie and I pick you up around six and we go to the meat and three for dinner?" said Brian.

"I would love that," said Maggie. "I had no idea what I was going to make for dinner tonight."

Maggie was sitting on the porch dressed in her black pants and red sweater when Brian and Jamie arrived. Brian hopped out of the car and opened the door for Maggie. "You look gorgeous," he whispered as he closed the door.

They took a small table in the back of the café. Maggie encouraged Jamie to eat some carrots and peas. Jamie said she liked carrots, but not peas so much. Maggie ordered chicken, baked potato and peas. She wanted to set a good example for Jamie. Jamie was eating while coloring a picture and not paying much attention to Brian and Maggie.

"Judge Parker sentenced John Butcher to an easy stint of fifteen years at Green Meadow Mental Institution," said Brian.

"At least he won't be around here," said Maggie.

"Yes, Green Meadow is at least a hundred miles away," said Brian.

As they were finishing up their meal with ice cream, Brian looked over at Jamie. "Do you think we should tell her our secret?" he asked.

"She already knows who I am," said Jamie. "Tell her who you are."

Maggie looked at Brian.

"This is a good day to come clean," he said. "My name is not Brian Scott."

"I already figured out your last name must be Turner," said Maggie.

184

"You're right about that. My real name is Stanley James Turner. Before I went into the CIA my friends called me Stan."

"CIA? I knew law enforcement, but never realized it was CIA. This is going to take some getting used to," said Maggie. "Are you using Stan at The Farm? I have a million questions, but I suppose I'm still not able to ask?"

"Most of what I've been doing is classified and it's really best if you don't know," said Stan. But from now on I'll just be dealing with the problems at The Farm. "There'll be no more name changes. I will not be chasing criminals. That life is behind me. I've decided I want a more settled life," said Stan.

"I'm glad," said Maggie, as Stan, Maggie and Jamie left the restaurant and drove back to Maggie's house.

"How's your daddy doing?" asked Stan.

"He's doing alright. I'll take him home this weekend. Mother is quitting work to stay home with him," said Maggie.

"Do you want me to ride up there with you?" asked Stan.

"That would be lovely," said Maggie.

"I had better get this school girl in bed," said Stan, as he tousled Jamie's hair.

"I'll call you about the time to leave on Friday evening," said Maggie.

"Ok, see you then," said Stan, as he and Jamie left. On the way home Stan and Jamie were talking.

"What would you think if I asked Maggie to marry me?" asked Stan.

"You mean Ms. Maggie would be my mommy?" asked Jamie.

"Yes, she would be my wife and your mommy and you could be her little girl, if you want to," said Stan. "It wouldn't mean she would take the place of your mommy. But, since your

mommy can't be here; she could be your mommy that's here."

"I love her so much," said Jamie. "I want her to be my mommy that's here."

"I love her so much, too," said Stan. "Don't say anything. I want it to be a surprise. Do you want to go with me tomorrow night to buy her an engagement ring?"

"Yes," said Jamie, "but what if she says no?"

"If she says no, we'll be very sad and I'll have to take the ring back, but I hope she says yes," said Stan.

"Me too," said Jamie, folding her hands as if to pray.

The next afternoon Stan and Jamie went to Clark Jewelry Store. Jamie was so excited. Right away he and Jamie saw the ring they wanted. It was an Edwardian white gold and platinum ruby and rose diamond cluster. Jamie said it was the most beautiful ring she had ever seen. It cost a little over two thousand dollars. The store owner said they had a payment plan, but Stan said he would just pay cash. He had worked hard over the years and had saved his money. He couldn't think of a better way to spend it.

When Friday came Avery was dismissed from the hospital, but Maggie couldn't pick him up until four. Stan arranged for Jamie to spend the weekend with Paula and met Maggie at her house to ride with her to take her daddy home. Avery looked pale and was quiet. "I just don't have any energy," he said.

"Maybe being home will help you feel better," said Maggie.

Lucy was excited to see them coming. She had dinner ready, fried chicken, okra and mashed potatoes. Avery asked about Jamie and said she would have liked the pulley bone. Maggie kidded and said that was her piece of chicken. Growing up she had always been given the best Avery could provide.

It was just getting dark when Maggie and Stan left Avery and Lucy sitting on their porch. Stan turned right and went in the direction of Lookout Point. He pulled the car to a stop. He and Maggie sat looking out over the landscape. The lights of Durant were beginning to glow. Stan put his arm around Maggie and pulled her close.

"Maggie, for almost a year now you've been my closest friend, you've been there for me when I needed comfort and when I shared my joys. You've been a friend to Jamie and helped her through the most hurtful time in her life. I've come to realize I want you in my life forever. You are much more than a friend. I've fallen in love with you and I want you to be my wife and a mother to Jamie. Will you marry me?"

"You've been my best friend this year. I always think of telling you when I have a problem or a joy. You mean so much to me. I love you, too. Yes, I'll marry you," said Maggie.

Stan reached into his pocket and pulled out a small box and opened it. "Jamie and I picked this out for you. I hope you like it," said Stan.

"It's so beautiful," Maggie said, as Stan slipped the ring on her finger and kissed her with passion that neither of them quite knew how to handle. "Maybe we should be going," said Stan.

"Yes," said Maggie, trying to breathe.

Stan turned on the jazz station and soon they were relaxed and at home. "I want to tell my parents," said Maggie. "Do you think we can go back up there tomorrow?"

"Of course," said Stan. "Our parents should be the first to know. Jamie already knows. I'll call my parents in the morning, but you're right, we should tell your daddy in person." Stan decided to stay the night, but Maggie made him sleep on the couch.

After breakfast they drove back to Boonetown. Avery was sitting in his chair by the living room door. Lucy was busy in the kitchen cleaning up the breakfast dishes.

"What're you two doing back here so soon?" asked Avery.

"We have an announcement to make," said Maggie, holding out her hand for Avery to see.

"Lucy, come in here," yelled Avery.

Lucy came running in. "What's wrong?" she asked, looking a little scared.

"These two young people have something to tell you," said Avery.

"We're going to get married," said Maggie, showing her mother her ring.

"That's pretty," said Lucy. "When's the big date?"

"We haven't had time to talk about that yet," said Maggie. "You'll be the first to know when we decide."

"Welcome to the family, son," said Avery to Stan. "Now what's your name?"

"My name is Stanley James Turner," said Stan. "My parents live in Missouri. I called them this morning and they're excited. Maggie has been up there with me several times. She was my little girl's teacher last year. That's how we met. You know Jamie's mother was George and Martha Anderson's daughter. I believe we met at the coroner's office when she died?"

"I remember," said Avery.

"The trial is over and we're trying to put all that sadness behind us and look ahead to happier times," said Stan.

"I'm happy for you," said Avery.

Lucy and Maggie went in the kitchen to talk leaving Avery and Stan to get acquainted. "Do you still have that government job?"

"Yes sir. I still work for the government, but I've taken a different job. I've decided to settle down and become a family man. I'm now the manager of The Farm," said Stan.

"Glad to hear it," said Avery.

Stan and Maggie stayed about an hour and left to pick up Jamie at Paula's house. Jamie was jumping up and down. "I'm so excited," she said, wrapping her arms around Maggie's waist.

"Me, too," said Maggie. "Let's go get ice cream to celebrate."

"Good idea," said Stan, as they drove toward the Dairy Queen. Eating their treat, they drove back to Maggie's house to plan a wedding.

Chapter 38

"First, let's set a date," said Maggie.

"When is fall break from school?" asked Stan.

Maggie looked on her school calendar. "It's October 12th through the 16th. We could get married on Friday or Saturday and have the whole next week before I have to go back to work," said Maggie, looking at Stan. "Is this a good time for you to be off?"

Stan pulled his scheduling calendar from his pocket. "Looks like nothing major that week. Let's get married on Sunday the 11th. We'll check to see if Jamie can spend the week with Paula and maybe we can go on a short honeymoon," said Stan.

"Alright, October 11th it is," said Maggie. "I don't think Daddy will be able to go anywhere and I want him at our wedding so we'll have the wedding in the yard at Mother and Daddy's house. The yard should be covered with yellow and orange maple leaves. It will make for a colorful fall setting. I'll figure it out, should we get the Reverend Robert Jones to perform the ceremony?"

"I think he would be appropriate considering all he's been through with us," said Stan.

"Will you be my best girl?" asked Maggie, looking at Jamie.

"Yes, yes," said Jamie. "Can I have a pretty pink dress?"

"You'll have the prettiest pink dress ever," said Maggie.

"Who should we invite," asked Stan.

"Your parents, George and Martha, Junior and Joe . . .

"Paula and her mother and daddy," interrupted Jamie.

"What about the Adams?" asked Stan.

"I'll call them, but I don't think they'll come," said Maggie. "I've only talked to them two or three times this year and that was when I called Mrs. Adams. They don't socialize much."

"I'll see if Junior can be my best man," said Stan.

"I like that," said Maggie. "I'll let Mother and Daddy know. You call Martha, George and Junior and I'll contact Joe and Reverend

Jones. Jamie are you ready to go shopping? We've got some dresses to buy!"

"Come on, Jamie. It's your bedtime," said Stan. "I need to get in the bed too, I've got a busy week ahead."

"I'm going to spend this coming Saturday with Mother and Daddy. While I'm there I'll start getting things together," said Maggie.

Maggie was glowing. She showed her ring off at school and soon the school was buzzing about her upcoming nuptials.

On Friday Maggie called her parents. "Is it alright if I come up and spend the night and part of the day tomorrow?" she asked.

"Glad to have you," said Avery. His voice was weak, but his spirit was strong.

Maggie arrived before dark and settled in to watch TV with her daddy. "While you're here tomorrow I think I'll run over to my sister's house for a while," said Lucy.

"That's a good idea," said Maggie. "Tell her she's invited to the wedding. See if she'll bring her keyboard and play the wedding march for me. We're not inviting many people."

"That's good, my sister doesn't like crowds," said Lucy. "But she can play the piano with the best of them."

"Tell her she'll feel right at home," said Maggie, as she kissed her daddy good night. He was tired so everyone went to bed early.

After a breakfast of ham, eggs, redeye gravy and biscuits Maggie told Lucy to go on over to her sister's house, she would do the dishes. Avery dressed and went to his chair where he fell sound asleep. Maggie finished the dishes and came and sat down beside him. Avery awoke and looked over at her. "You're here," he said.

"Yes, I'm here," said Maggie.

"I have something I need to tell you," Avery said. "I've kept this secret for over thirty years. Only two other people know."

"Are you sure you want to tell me?" said Maggie.

"Yes, it's the right time. You need to know," said Avery. "Jenny was my daughter. I was too young to take responsibility for a child, so Martha married George. George doesn't know and Lucy doesn't know. Only Joe and Martha know. It would kill George if he found out. He was a good daddy to my little girl. Joe and I were living together when it happened. We shared almost everything when we were young."

Maggie was quiet. "So, Jamie is my niece?"

"Yes, that beautiful little girl is my granddaughter and your niece," said Avery.

"I've always known we have a special connection. Even from the first time we met there was something about her that touched me," said Maggie.

"There's no need to tell the others. You may want to tell Jamie when she's old enough to understand," said Avery. George has been my friend for many years. He loves Jamie and she loves him. It wouldn't benefit anybody if we told."

"I think you're right," said Maggie. "I will not tell anyone, not even Stan until the time is right. Jamie means the world to me and now that I know she's family she'll mean even more. I can't wait to be her mommy."

"And, a good mommy you'll be. You've always loved children and put them first," said Avery.

"I'm really tired. I think I'll lie down," said Avery. Maggie helped him up and gave him a hug. "Thanks for telling me," she said. "It's a lot to think about. It would have been nice to have known my sister, but I understand why you didn't tell. At least I'll have her daughter in my life. She's a wonderful little girl."

Lucy came running through the door. "What have you gotten done on the wedding?" she asked. "Polly said she'll play the keyboard for you."

"I called Reverend Jones and he will officiate, and we can borrow a few chairs from the church. He'll bring them when he comes. And he has one of those arches that we can put flowers on and stand in front of. Joe said he'll come. Jamie and I are going shopping next Saturday for our dresses. Mother, what are you wearing? Do you want me to buy you a new dress?" asked Maggie.

"No, I have that pink lace dress not many people have seen," said Lucy.

"Perfect," said Maggie. "Jamie is wearing pink and I'll carry baby pink roses in my bouquet. Daddy can just wear his gray suit. We're all homefolk and friends."

When Maggie arrived home, Stan called. "Junior is coming to be my best man and my parents are coming. Junior was a little surprised. I never told him we were dating. Paula's mom said she would be happy to watch Jamie for a few days," said Stan.

"You got a lot done. I've arranged for Reverend Jones and Aunt Polly will play the keyboard for us," said Maggie.

"I'm going to have to work next weekend so I can be off the following weekend and week. Do you think Jamie can stay with you?" asked Stan.

"Jamie and I need to go shopping on Saturday morning and we can go up to be with Daddy on Saturday afternoon and finish arranging for a cake and some punch. There's a neighbor who likes to cater small gatherings. I'll call her," said Maggie.

"Jamie will love spending time with your daddy," said Stan.

"He'll love it, too. He loves children," said Maggie.

"What's for dinner? Can we come over tonight?" asked Stan.

"I'll make hamburgers, French fries and peas," said Maggie.

"We'll be right over," said Stan.

Stan worked overtime all week getting things caught up so he could take a week off. On Saturday morning he brought Jamie and her pajamas over to Maggie's house. Jamie skipped in and put her bag in the spare bedroom. Stan hurried to The Farm. Maggie and Jamie were soon shopping for their dresses. Maggie chose an ivory, short-sleeved, pearl studded V-neck satin gown. Jamie's pink dress was overlaid with chiffon. They stopped by Maggie's house to leave their dresses before heading to Boonetown to spend time with Maggie's daddy and mother.

"We're going to be so pretty," said Maggie.

"I'm glad you're going to be my mommy that's here," said Jamie.

"I'm excited to be your mommy that's here," said Maggie.

"Is Mr. Avery your daddy like Stan is my daddy?" asked Jamie.

"Yes, Mr. Avery is my daddy," said Maggie.

"What do I call him? Do I call him Mr. Avery?" asked Jamie.

"You can call him Mr. Avery if you want to, but since he's my daddy and I'll be your mommy that's here, you could call him Papa Avery," said Maggie.

"I like Papa Avery. I'll have three papas; Papa George, Papa James and now Papa Avery. It's fun having three papas," said Jamie.

"You're very fortunate," said Maggie, as they pulled into the Sutton driveway.

Maggie and Jamie entered the living room. "Hi Daddy, how're you feeling today?" asked Maggie.

"I'm alright. Just a little tired," said Avery. "Hello Jamie. How're you?" said Avery.

"I'm good," said Jamie, carrying her book, crayons and paper to put them on the coffee table where she sat down on the floor and began drawing.

"Where's mother?" asked Maggie.

"She's back there is the kitchen somewhere," said Avery.

Maggie proceeded to go to the kitchen to find her mother. She wanted to ask her about the neighbor who did catering. Jamie continued to draw.

"What are you drawing?" asked Avery.

"Our family," said Jamie.

"Let me see," said Avery.

"This is Daddy, this is Mommy Maggie, and Papa Avery, this is you," said Jamie.

"So that's me," said Avery, with a tear running down his face. "That looks just like me."

Maggie was gone for about ten minutes getting the refreshments for the wedding reception arranged. When she returned to the living room Jamie was sitting in Avery's lap reading to him. *I Loved You Since Forever* by Suzie Mason. "You and I turned into we," read Jamie. "The End." The joy Maggie felt was overwhelming. She went outside to get her breath. When it was time to go Jamie gave Avery a goodbye kiss. They had become immediate friends.

The wedding was in a week. The front yard was filling up with a blanket of yellow and orange. Reverend Robby Jones brought the archway and placed it in the middle of the yard. Chairs were placed on either side of a mowed clean aisle. Excitement was building. Maggie and Jamie would spend Saturday night with Lucy and Avery. Stan and Junior would come on Sunday. Maggie picked the flowers up from the florist and put them in the refrigerator for safekeeping. Jamie slept with Maggie, but neither of them slept much. They kept giggling and talking. Lucy threatened to give them both a spanking. It seemed like forever, but it was morning. Stan and Junior arrived about 12:30. The wedding was scheduled for 2:00.

The decorating was done. The guests were sitting in their places. Maggie and Jamie were in the backroom dressing. Lucy's sister was sitting at the keyboard. Junior and Stan took their places in front of the arch.

The wedding march sounded. Maggie and Jamie rushed to the living room. Maggie looked out and saw Avery sitting with Lucy holding hands on the front row. Stan's parents were on the other side of the aisle. Maggie nudged Jamie. "Go, you're first," she said. Jamie began walking slowly down the grassy aisle strewing rose petals as she went. When she reached Stan she stopped and he stooped down and kissed her. Maggie followed stopping to kiss her mother and daddy. Stan reached for her hand and they stood before Reverend Jones to take their vows. It was a short ceremony ending with the exchanging of rings. "With this ring I thee wed," said Stan, as he placed a matching wedding band on Maggie's finger. Maggie had purchased a plain gold band for Stan. "With this ring I thee wed," she said.

"I now pronounce you husband and wife," said Reverend Jones. "You may kiss your bride." Everyone clapped and threw rice, as the couple ran down the aisle to the front porch. Reverend Jones said, "There's cake and punch for everyone. Have fun." Stan and Maggie went over to the table and cut the cake, feeding each other, laughing. Jamie and Paula came over to get cake. Lucy's sister played and sang *For Once in My Life*. She wasn't half bad. Maggie and Stan danced. Maggie looked over at her daddy as he stood and took Lucy into his arms to dance, but Avery had to sit down before the song was over. Maggie remembered her daddy told her it was dancing that brought her parents together.

"We had better change our clothes and be on our way," said Stan. Maggie had no idea where they were going, but she knew who she was going with and that was all that mattered. Junior and Reverend Jones said they would clean up.

Maggie and Stan kissed Jamie goodbye and Maggie went over to her daddy, "You take care of yourself while I'm gone," she said. "I'll call you every day."

"I'll try," said Avery.

Maggie and Stan drove away headed for Florida with tin cans dragging behind the Camaro with a 'Just Married' sign in the back window.

"We'll stop for dinner before we get to our motel," said Stan. "We can take the sign down and dispose of the tin cans then." Stan turned the radio on. Ella Fitzgerald was singing For *Once in My Life*.

The motel was ordinary, but Maggie and Stan failed to notice. Both of them had had sex before, but tonight they made love. They had found peace and happiness that neither of them had known existed.

On Monday afternoon Maggie and Stan pulled into the parking lot of their motel in Pensacola, Florida. The white sandy beach was inviting, and the ocean breeze was enticing. They were soon in their bathing suits out for a run on the beach. "This is living the dream," said Stan, as he pulled a beach chair up beside Maggie handing her a cool drink.

"I love it," said Maggie.

"I had two reasons for picking this place for our honeymoon," said Stan. First, I wanted to bring you somewhere you'd never been. You told me once you'd never seen the ocean and the second reason is my friend moved here. Tomorrow I want us to run by to see him. I want you to meet him."

"I really would like to meet him," said Maggie. "Is he married?"

"No, he's one of those guys who has devoted his entire life to the CIA," said Stan. "Family is not encouraged."

"Speaking of family, can we charge phone calls to our room?"

"Yes, I believe we can. Do you want to check on your daddy?"

"I want to check on Daddy and Jamie. We won't have to talk long," said Maggie.

"We'd better go in soon. I think I'm getting blistered," said Stan.

"You won't blister. You just turn brown. I'm the one who turns red," said Maggie, laughing. They packed up their gear and went inside. Maggie reached in her purse and pulled out Paula's number. "I hope they're not eating dinner," she said. "This is Maggie Turner; may I speak with Jamie?" said Maggie.

"Hello," said Jamie.

"Hi sweetheart, it's Mommy Maggie. How are you?"

"I'm ok. Paula and I have been working puzzles," said Jamie.

"I'm glad you're having fun. We're having fun, too. We'll see you soon. Here, say hi to your daddy," said Maggie.

"Hi Daddy," said Jamie.

"I love you," said Stan. "Behave yourself and we'll see you soon."

"I will," said Jamie. "I'll see you soon. Bye."

"One more call and we'll have the evening to ourselves," said Maggie. "Maybe we can go to that club on the corner and dance. It was fun dancing at our wedding."

"Sounds like a plan," said Stan.

Maggie picked up the phone and rang her parents' number. Lucy's sister answered the phone.

"Aunt Polly?" asked Maggie.

"Yes, honey it's me. Your mother's in no shape to talk on the phone," said Polly.

"What's wrong?" asked Maggie.

"It's your daddy, honey. He died this morning," said Polly.

Maggie couldn't speak. She handed the phone to Stan. "Polly, what's wrong?" asked Stan.

"Avery just up and died this morning without any warning. Lucy found him lying on the floor by his chair. He was gone. There was nothing she could do," said Polly.

"Tell Lucy we'll be home as soon as we can get there. We're in Florida. It'll take us all night, but we'll come straight home," said Stan. He hung the phone up and took Maggie into his arms and let her cry. "We'll grab some sandwiches and take them with us. I want you to rest. I'll drive."

Maggie sobbed until her tears were dry and she finally fell asleep. Stan drove faster than usual. He wanted Maggie to be with Lucy by morning. He pulled into the Sutton driveway at 6:00 a.m. It appeared everyone was still asleep. Maggie roused. "Are we here?" she asked.

"Yeah, but I don't think they're up yet," said Stan.

"Let's wait until we see lights come on," said Maggie. At 6:30 the first lights flickered. Maggie jumped out of the car and ran toward the house. Stan was right behind her.

"Mother, Mother, I'm here," cried Maggie, as she cradled Lucy in her arms.

"He was here one minute and gone the next," said Lucy.

"It's so hard," said Maggie. Polly came into the room announcing breakfast. She had prepared biscuits, ham and eggs. The coffee smelled divine. Stan poured everyone a cup of coffee and they sat down to eat. "It's important to eat," said Polly.

"Yes," said Maggie. "Thank you for all that you're doing."

After breakfast Lucy and Maggie began planning Avery's funeral. "Reverend Jones will officiate," said Lucy. "And I want the quartet

Avery liked to sing his favorite song, 'Life's Evening Sun'. He'll be buried in the Sutton cemetery with his daddy, mother and brothers."

"When is the funeral?" asked Stan.

"Day after tomorrow at 5:30 p.m.," said Lucy. We'll have visitation tomorrow night from 6:00 until 8:00. I'll sit up with him until midnight."

"I'll stay there with you," said Maggie. "I want to go as far as I can go with him. He has supported me in everything I've ever done."

"I couldn't have asked for a better husband," said Lucy. "Oh, we had our ups and downs, but who doesn't?"

"The church is adjacent to the cemetery and it's going to be a beautiful fall day for the burial. I believe the sun sets around 5:48. Daddy always said he wanted to be buried at sunset," said Maggie.

"In the morning, I'll go get Jamie and bring her here," said Stan.

"Yes," said Maggie. "It's important for children to be included in the sad times as well as the happy times."

The following day Stan brought Jamie to be with the family when they went to the funeral home to choose a casket for Avery. Lucy took his gray suit for him to wear. Maggie picked a blue and yellow tie she had seen her daddy wear so many times.

On the day of the funeral, Avery's body was brought to the church where Reverend Jones told stories about Avery hunting and how God had blessed him with a loving family and how he had attained a better hunting ground and an everlasting home not made with hands. His nephews accompanied Avery to the cemetery and carried his body to the grave site. Joe and Junior were at the funeral, but didn't participate in the service.

Lucy dressed in black with the yellow scarf she had received from Avery for her birthday. She sat on the front row beside Maggie across from the now closed casket. Maggie and Stan sat holding hands, with Jamie sitting on Stan's knee. The extraordinary sunset was the perfect backdrop for the Cessna 182 B Skylane flying near the Jungle.

The quartet was singing: *Life's evening sun is sinking low; it is time and I must go. To meet the deeds that I have done where there will be no setting sun.*

About the Author

Nancy Evelyn Allen is the author of the award-winning "Covenant Woman" series, has published over 200 "Little Stories about You and Me", 87 vignettes for radio and has stories in Anthologies and Magazines. She has a BS degree from Tennessee Technological University and a MA degree from Southern Baptist Theological Seminary. She and her husband have been married for 61 years. They have two children, three grandchildren and five great-grandchildren.